# THE NOTHING to see HERE
## ***HOTEL***
# SEA-ING IS Believing!

**STEVEN BUTLER**

**ILLUSTRATED BY STEVEN LENTON**

SIMON & SCHUSTER

For the very magical Rainer Starr Stoyer.
You're always welcome at the
Nothing To See Here Hotel.

From Steven and Steven ... and Nancy x

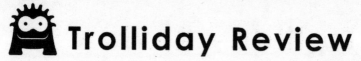

# Trolliday Review

You are viewing user reviews for The Nothing To See Here Hotel, Brighton

## The Nothing To See Here Hotel

NB. Everyone is welcome at The Nothing to See Here Hotel (except humans... NEVER HUMANS!)

🎃🎃🎃🎃🎃 1,079 Reviews   #1 of 150 Hotels in Brighton

📍 Brighton Seafront UK BN1 1NTSH   📞 00 11 2 334 4556   ✉ E-mail hotel

---

**Francesca Simon**

🎃🎃🎃🎃🎃 Reviewed 2 days ago

'A rip-roaring, swashbuckling, amazerous magical adventure. Comedy gold.'

---

**Jeremy Strong**

🎃🎃🎃🎃🎃 Reviewed 13 days ago

'A splundishly swashbungling tale of trolls, goblins and other bonejangling creatures. Put on your wellies and plunge into the strangest hotel you will ever encounter. This is a hotel I hope I never find! Wonderfully, disgustingly funny.'

---

**Cressida Cowell**

🎃🎃🎃🎃🎃 Reviewed 29 days ago

'Hilariously funny and inventive, and I love the extraordinary creatures and the one thirty-sixth troll protagonist...'

---

**Frank Cottrell Boyce**

🎃🎃🎃🎃🎃 Reviewed 205 days ago

'Weirdly hilarious and hilariously weird!'

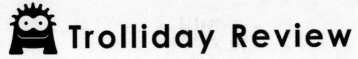

# Trolliday Review

**You are viewing user reviews for The Nothing To See Here Hotel, Brighton**

# The Nothing To See Here Hotel

NB. Everyone is welcome at The Nothing to See Here Hotel (except humans... NEVER HUMANS!)

1,079 Reviews   #1 of 150 Hotels in Brighton

Brighton Seafront UK BN1 1NTSH   00 11 2 334 4556   E-mail hotel

---

**Liz
Pichon**

Reviewed 33 days ago

'This hotel gets five slimey stars from me...'

---

**Jacqueline
Wilson**

Reviewed 54 days ago

'A magical hotel, known for its exclusive unique clientele. The chef is to be congratulated for inventing Bizarre Cuisine. All staff very friendly, but avoid the Manager (especially if you're wearing a cat-suit).'

---

**Kaye
Umansky**

Reviewed 75 days ago

'What a fun hotel! Book me in immediately!'

1   DINNER IN THE DARK

2   MALONEY'S GIFT

3   THE SKELL-A-PHONE KEY

4   A FAMILY REUNION

5   A GHAST FROM THE PAST

6   CURIOUS GUESTS

7   PANDEMONIUM

8   DON'T MESS WITH MAUDLIN MALONEY

9   THE FOURTH KEYHOLE

10   WELCOME UNDER

11   THE ATILANTUS

12   WHOOMMFF!!

**13** OH, I DO LIKE TO BE BENEATH THE SEASIDE!

 **14** THE BRINY BALLROOM

 **15** SOMETHING A LITTLE BIT STRANGE

 **16** ABRAHAM'S OFFICE

 **17** TREASURES IN THE COBWEBS

 **18** THE GRAVEGHAST'S CURSE

**19** PHEWY!!

 **20** TIME TO CELEBRATE!

 **21** HIDING FROM CHORES

 **22** THE GRAND RE-OPENING

 **23** THE BOTTOM OF THE SEA BALL

 **24** WHAAAAAAATT!?!?

WELCOME TO

# THE N☉THING to see HERE HOTEL

 **THE SPEECH**

 **SEEING DOUBLE**

 **A SPECTRIL'S REVENGE!**

 **GUNDISKUMP!**

 **THE RACE TO DRY LAND**

 **KA-BOOM!**

 **THAT'S THAT THEN...**

MAGICALS WELCOME! **HOTEL** BRIGHTON, UK

THE NOTHING TO
SEE HERE HOTEL

Brighton S

MAGICALS WELCOME! **HOTEL** BRIGHTON, UK

THE NOTHING TO
SEE HERE HOTEL

Brighton Seafront

UK

BN1 1NTSH

Are you in need of a relaxing getaway or somewhere to escape the daily grind of lair lurking, bridge bothering or humdrum haunts? **The Nothing to See Here Hotel** is the place for you. We take honkhumptious pride in being the best secret holiday destination for magical creatures in the whole of England.

Whether it's soaking your scales in our pool, sampling the toothsome delicacies created by our spider-cook extraordinaire, Nancy (her porcupaties smothered in sticky giblet jam are to die for), reading up on a curse or two in the library, or just cooling your bunions at our luxurious mud spa, we

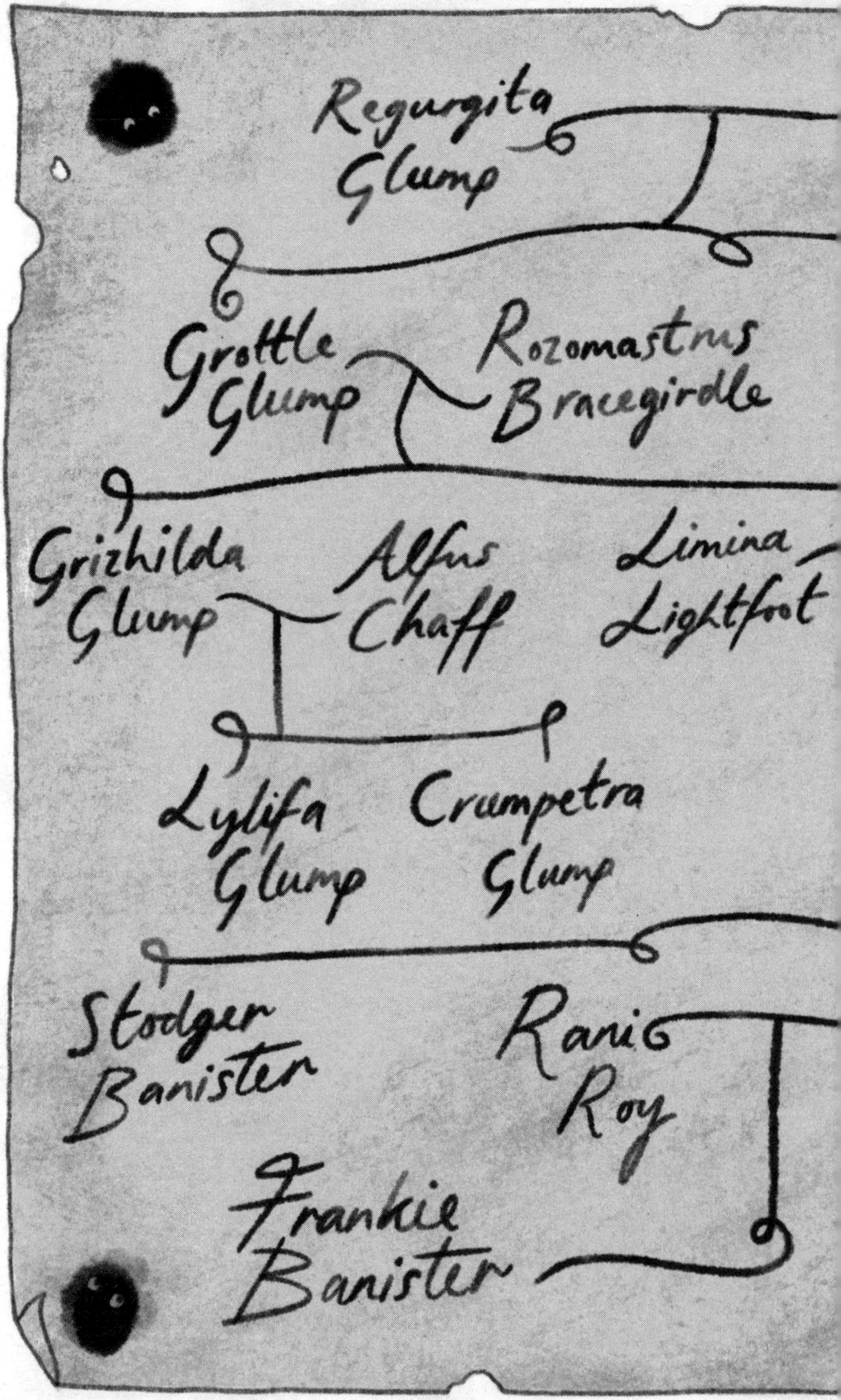

Regurgita
Glump

Grottle
Glump

Rozomastus
Bracegirdle

Grizhilda
Glump

Alfus
Chaff

Limina
Lightfoot

Lylifa
Glump

Crumpetra
Glump

Stodger
Banister

Ranis
Roy

Frankie
Banister

Abraham Banister — Olympia Nocturne

Zennifer Glump

Oculus Nocturne

Ignotius Glump

Tussely Banister — Blundus Glump

Festus M'Gurk — Bombastis Banister

Bargeous Banister

Markle Banister

The Banister Family Tree

## DINNER IN THE DARK

'Hurry up and get this blunkin' thing over with!' my great-great-great-granny, Regurgita Glump, growled as she plonked her gargantuan bottom across three kitchen chairs with a painful creak. 'I can't be botherin' with stupidly nonkumbumps all night!'

'Och, come now, my deary,' Nancy said from the stove. She carried a pot of shrimp-scale tea over to the table and placed it among the plates of badger-milk buns and crispy fried mudwump fritters smothered in spicy mango chutney. 'It's a wee dinner party. It's going to be lovely!'

My grunion of a granny scowled around the room at all of us. Her hulking frame took up one whole side of the kitchen table, and in the dim light she was a nightmare to behold. Her piggy eyes glinted copper and her nose scrunched up like she'd just caught the whiff of something disgusterous.

'Ch-ch-cheer up, Granny,' I stammered. It was at times like these I wished I wasn't one-quarter magical… that way I wouldn't be able to see so clearly in the dark. It'd be lovely not to have to look at her grizzly lumpish face.

'You can bog right off if you think I'm getting all jiggery and festivous!' the old troll grunted. 'I'm only here for the food, make no mistakings!' Then she scooped up a huge fistful of rattle-snitch sausages and stuffed them into her gaping gob, slobbering and drooling like a honking great hog in a stained nightdress.

'Well,' Mum said from the far end of the table. 'It's been a funny old summer, hasn't it? But that's not going to stop us celebrating Abraham's birthday.'

'Exactly!' Dad added as he took a seat next to her. 'It's only right that we have our little shindig in his honour.'

Mum turned to me and smiled a slightly nervous smile.

'Just like old times!' Nancy beamed as she brought over an enormous birthday cake, covered in bright-green seagull snot frosting and dotted with squillions of candles, placing it right in the middle of the spread.

If my great-great-great-grandad, Abraham Bannister, was still alive, it would be his one hundred and seventy-fifth birthday tomorrow. Every year, on the actual day, we have a big party with all our hotel guests to mark the anniversary, but on the night before, my family and our nearest and dearest always gather in the kitchen like this to raise a quiet toast of frog-grog to the old fellow.

'Just like old times!' Mum and Dad echoed. '**HAPPY BIRTHDAY, ABE!**'

The truth is, though … it didn't feel like old times – **NOT AT ALL.** This little party felt super strange and was making me more uncomfortable than the day Dad had to ask Lady Mulch, queen of the compost pooks, to leave because of all the bad smell complaints from our customers.

Righty … before we get stuck in, I think I owe you an explanation.

In case we haven't already met, my name is Frankie Banister. **HELLO!** If you have read any of my books, you'll know that my home is one of the best holiday destinations for magical creatures in the whole world, **the Nothing To See Here Hotel.** It's been in the family ever since my great-great-great-grandparents built it over one hundred years ago, and these days I run about with my mum, Rani, and my dad, Bargeous, trying to stop our constant flow of bonkers customers from demolishing it!

You might also know **ALL** about what's been going on lately. Things have been **MEGA-CRAZY ... EVEN MORE THAN USUAL ...** and that's saying something when you live in a place where weird is normal!

**BUT!!!** If you haven't heard any of my stories before, you'll be scratching your head and wondering what on earth I'm going on about.

Well, just read on and I'll tell you **EVERYTHING** quicker than you can yell, '**HONKSWALLOP!**'

You see ... so far this summer my family have faced pirate battles and leprechaun curses, and ginormous, plummety falls, and minkle-meatballs that tasted like dryad droppings, and freak blizzards, and families of yetis, and ferocious lightning storms, and battalions of goblin guards, and our unfortunate guests nearly being eaten by colossal shrunken heads, and thickets of gnashing thorns, and the statue of my Great-Great-Aunt Zennifer magically coming back to life in the foyer fountain, and talking magpies, and giant boulders exploding up through the garden … **AND THOSE ARE JUST THE LITTLE BITS!!**

Top all that off with watching a spoiled goblin prince accidentally being grunched-up by Mrs Venus, the giant fly-trap plant, and you're getting warmer … but that's not nearly the end of it.

Just when we thought things couldn't get any more noggin-bonked, my long-lost great-great-uncle, Oculus Nocturne, arrived unexpectedly and tried to destroy everything by breaking our invisibility spells and exposing **the Nothing To See Here Hotel** to the outside world! He also told us some terrible things about Grandad Abraham being a coward and a great big fibster, and now I didn't know what to think about all this celebrating stuff. Abe had always been a hero to me, but suddenly I wasn't so sure he should be.

It feels like our lives have been turned upside down and shaken about, and my parents seem to be

making things even more scrambled, I swear!

Ever since my great-great-uncle was carted off to be stored away at the top of the Himalayas inside a block of ice, Mum and Dad have been in frantic overdrive. They refuse to believe the rumours about Grandad Abe, and haven't stopped worrying what all our customers will think about the scandal.

It doesn't help that magicals are **SO NOSY!** With our enchanted wallpaper, it barely took a minute after Oculus was frozen before our guests had heard the stories whispering through the walls and they've been gossiping ever since. Talk of Abe being a big imposter, or a hero, or a complete wimpus has been a hot topic around the pool and in the mud spa.

So Mum and Dad have been cooing and pampering our guests more than **EVER** lately to try and distract them. Mum's even hired a permanent team of home-sweet-home hobs who scrub and mop and fix and make the beds for that extra bit of luxury. You can't put your mug of hot chunklet down for more than three seconds before the hobs have cleared it away. I've never seen the hotel so clean and tidy!

Anyway … fast-forward three weeks from the Oculus drama and here we were, sitting in the dark around the kitchen table, ready to celebrate the anniversary of Great-Great-Great-Grandad Abe's birthday, and I was feeling very confused indeed.

'Och, it looks beauteous!' Nancy chuckled. 'Even if I do say so myself.' She clapped her four hands together and fluttered her eight sets of eyelashes cheerfully. 'A feast for the family!'

Oh … I forgot. This is probably a good time to tell you that Nancy is a spider. A massive Orkney Brittle-back to be precise … **SURPRISE!** She's worked at the hotel ever since it opened and is practically part of the family.

'Well, then…' Dad said, looking around at our glowing faces in the candlelight. 'Who wants to say a few words?'

'I will!' beamed Nancy, raising her glass of bluebottle brandy. 'To Mr Banister! Without you and our dear Regurgita, we wouldn't be living in this lovely hotel.'

**'BLEEUUGH!'** Granny scoffed, but we all ignored her and clinked our cups and mugs together.

'To Abraham!' Mum said.

Dad gave me a cheerful nod, but I shrugged and stayed silent, so he turned his attention to the raggedy troll, scowling on the other side of the table. 'Regurgita, would you like to say a few words?'

'What?' my troll granny snapped, spitting a half-chewed sticklefish nugget across the room.

'Why don't you say something nice about Abe?

He was your husband, after all,' Dad said, trying to smile encouragingly. 'Just speak from the heart.'

Granny Regurgita looked at Dad as if he'd been talking jibberish or had just started flapping around the kitchen like an over-excited rooster.

'**SPEAK FROM THE HEART!?!?**' Granny suddenly cackled with laughter. '**WHAT A DUNGLISH THING TO BE GLUBBER GRUNTING ON ABOUT, BARGEOUS!**'

Dad's face fell into a frown.

'Abe Banister was a grobskwonking old gonk,' Granny continued with a wicked grin. 'Oh, he was a dreaderous husband! As useless as a chuffer in a bungle-box! Always jabbering on about blurty things like love and family and calling me "**SCHMOOPSY POO!**" and other rottly garbunk!'

'Those are lovely things!' Nancy said, reaching across the table and helping herself to a dandruff-dusted doughnut. 'It sounds very nice to me, my wee lamb.'

'Nice? **NICE?**' Granny scoffed. 'He wasn't so nice when he slunkered off like a sluglet and left me alone to manage this muck-dump on my own, was he?'

'But, Granny, Abe didn't abandon you, he ... popped his clonkers,' Mum mumbled. 'It's natural—'

'Natural? It's not natural, it's inconsiderate!! That clunkerous skrunt bogged off and left me here in this poodly hole with you bunch of scumlies!!'

I caught sight of Mum rolling her eyes in the gloom and nearly laughed out loud. Being completely human, she often forgets that even in near-total darkness our troll eyes can see her as clearly as if it was day.

'DON'T YOU ROLL YOUR EYES AT ME, RANI!' Granny blurted, as Mum's face twitched with horror. 'You're not too old for a smack on the bumly-bits, donchaknow? You can all coo and cudd-lump about that old blunker, but I'm not getting slobberchopsy, that's for sure!'

By now, my parents were staring with mouths wide open at my gruesome grandma. Dad even forgot he was crunching on a crab-shell-crostini, and it fell out from between his teeth, landing in his mug of tea with a loud **PLOP!**

**'THAT OLD SKUNKUS WAS A LILY-LIVERED LUMPLING! HE WAS A GRIM-HEARTED GURNIP! A SWINDLE-SWIZZLER! ABRAHAM BANISTER WAS A-'**

I think my great-great-great-granny could have gone on for ever if she hadn't been suddenly silenced by the kitchen door bursting open and Maudlin Maloney hobbling her way inside.

'Started without Manky Old Maloney, did you?' the ancient leprechaun croaked with a crooked leer. 'I might have known.'

## 2

## MALONEY'S GIFT

If you're new to all this, my human friend, you're probably wondering who on earth Maudlin Maloney is, right? And if you already know, you'll be thinking, **'OH, NO! NOT THAT CANTUNKEROUS OLD GRIZZLER!'**

Well, in case you don't already know, Miss Maloney is an exceptionally bad-tempered leprechaun who came to stay with us earlier in the summer. It's a bit embarrassing really, but shortly after she arrived I may have accidentally accused the grumpy bad luck fairy of trying to destroy the hotel instead of my Uncle Oculus.

But it was an honest mistake, I swear!

After all the craziness was over, we offered Manky Old Maloney a permanent place to stay in the hotel for free … y'know … to say sorry.

She ended up pitching her chicken-powered lepre-caravan in the corner of the foyer and now runs a gift shop from it, selling lucky trinkets and not-so-lucky curses to hotel guests. Her nostril-hair hex to deter nosy neighbours is going down a storm at the moment.

Just last week Gladys Potts, the werepoodle, used a jar of the stuff on a greedy garden garvil who'd

been snooping around the spot where she buries her best juicy bones in the flowerbeds. In three seconds flat, the little pest had sprouted dreadlocks from his hooter that were so long he kept tripping himself up. **HA!**

Anyway, where was I? Oh, yes…

○ ◯ ○

'Don't even think about eatin' all that birthday cake without saving a gobbleful for me and my girls!' Maloney chuckled as she clomped her way over to the table, followed by a few of her pet chickens, clucking and *B-KERKING* as they straggled behind her.

The bad luck fairy hauled herself up onto the chair next to me. No one had the courage to tell her she hadn't been invited to the dinner party … not even Granny Regurgita, so we all just smiled.

'What are we having?' she grinned, showing a set of teeth as grey and wonky as gravestones. 'Nancy, be a dunkling and pass me a porcupatty, would you?'

Nancy handed Maudlin the platter of patties in silence and the little leprechaun snatched at them greedily. She opened up her full mouth to speak again between chews, then stopped herself as she finally noticed the exasperated look on my parents' faces, and my scowling granny, who'd taken to biting huge chunks out of her plate in anger.

'Ha! I smell a family squabble,' the leprechaun smirked. 'What's the problem? Boggles in the basement? Night-gorms under the bed? Skullery blights in the kitchen cupboards?'

'Not exactly,' Mum groaned.

'What's happening, then? Tell Old Maloney, she'll fix it for you, so she will.'

'It's just that we're trying to have a nice little party for Abe's birthday,' said Dad. 'And … and …'

**'AND I SAID HE'S SLUDGEROUS SLOB-GLOB!'** Granny Regurgita interrupted.

'Oh, I see,' said Maloney, scratching the whiskers on her chin.

'He isn't!' Dad blurted, trying his best to look as stern as possible. 'The rumours about Abraham aren't true. He's always been the pride of our family and a real hero. Oculus was spreading lies, that's all!

I just know it!'

## 'ABRAHAM WAS A FOOZLE FART!'

'No, he wasn't!'

I'd never seen Dad stand up to Granny Regurgita like this before. I couldn't tell if I felt proud of him or scared for his safety. I'd seen my troll-granny bowl people straight through walls for far less than answering back.

'Well, it looks like I came just in the nick of time, then, doesn't it?' Maudlin said, interrupting the argument. **'OLD MALONEY SAVES THE DAY AGAIN.'**

'I'm sorry?' Mum said. 'I don't know what you mean.'

I glanced at the stumpy bad luck fairy in the candlelight and could tell she was up to something. A mischievous grin had spread across her face and there was a glint of naughtiness in her eyes.

'I've got a winkly present for you all!' Maloney beamed, rubbing her gnarled hands together. 'Oh, ho ho, it's a good'un! I've been saving this for yonks and yonkers!'

With that, Maudlin turned to her chickens, who had been chasing Granny's pet thistlewump, Gurp, around the floor, and yelled, **'QUICK, GIRLS! WHICH ONE OF YOU HAS IT? CLAWDELIA? HENELOPE? LADY CLUCK?'**

A plump black-and-white chicken flapped up to the table and perched clumsily on the lid of the teapot. In its beak, I could see something small and

twisty, like a bent piece of copper wire…

'AH, EGGWINA! OF COURSE!' Maloney cooed, holding out her three-fingered hand. The bird dropped whatever it was clutching into the leprechaun's palm then flapped back to the kitchen floor in a flurry of feathers. 'Let's show 'em what we've brought!'

## THE SKELL-A-PHONE KEY

'**TA-DAH!**' Maudlin hooted, flourishing her hand at us. Between two of her stumpy fingers, she was holding what looked like a little white marble attached to a thin, twisty piece of metal with tiny notches and teeth cut into it, sort of like a key. 'Hows about that, then?'

Nobody spoke.

'Umm, thank you, Maudlin,' said Mum, after a silence that seemed to go on for ever. 'It's lovely.'

'Is it a...?' Dad mumbled. 'It's a ... errr ... it's definitely ... what is it?'

Maloney grimaced. 'I don't know why I bother sometimes!' she grumbled. 'Honestly! What kind of brain-bungled eejits don't know a skell-a-phone key when they see one?'

'A skell-a-what?' Mum asked, looking embarrassed.

**'A SKELL-A-PHONE KEY!'**
Maudlin barked. 'Worth a small blunkin' fortune. I had to haggle with a hitchy-scratch for hours to get me hands on it, so I did!'

'Och, how lovely, dear!' Nancy said, leaning in for a better look. 'But I'm not sure I've ever heard of one.'

'Me neither,' said Dad.

'What's it for?' I asked, and instantly regretted it.

'See for yourself, boy.' Maudlin turned her piercing gaze on me and I felt a shudder creep across my skin. Even though the ancient leprechaun had become a close friend of the family since she saved our lives a few weeks back, I still found her super spine-jangling. 'It'll curl your toes with shock.'

She held the skell-a-phone key out towards me

and I nervously took the small object.

'It's not dangerous, is it?' Mum whimpered as I turned the strange thing over in my hand.

'Depends on who's using it,' Maudlin cackled.

Getting a closer look, I saw for the first time that what I thought was a white marble was actually an ornately carved little skull, and the strip of intricately notched and twisted metal sticking out of its base had tiny letters engraved into it.

'"Gimble and Gump's Otherworldly Supplies",' I read out loud.

'They're the best makers of skell-a-phone keys in all the worlds,' Maloney declared, looking very proud indeed.

'But …' Mum looked terrified to ask. 'What does it do?'

'**HA HA!**' Maudlin snatched the key back from me and bounded off her chair. 'I'll show you, Rani,' she guffawed excitedly. 'You'll love it, so you will.'

We all watched in wide-eyed silence as the leprechaun hobbled across the kitchen, scattering her chickens in all directions. She headed straight to the yell-a-phone that hung on the wall next to the fireplace, then stopped and grinned back at us.

'After all the gossipy grumble-griping that's been going on about Abraham Banister, I say we ask him ourselves and find out the truth once and for all. Let's see if he really did run off and leave his one-eyed bratling to be gruzzled by a graveghast!'

In no time, everyone was huddled around, waiting to see what Maudlin's gadget could do. Well, everyone except Granny Regurgita. She refused to show any interest and was so annoyed when we all left the table, she took to grabbing fistfuls of food from our plates.

'Rumblish nonkumbumps, if you ask me!' the greedy troll slurped between mouthfuls of birthday cake and squirrel-cheese twirls. 'You'll be sorry … I'll gobble the lot!'

I suppose now would be a good moment to tell you what a yell-a-phone is, just in case you don't know, my human friend. The yell-a-phone is an irritating contraption that allows us to speak to anyone around the building, no matter where they are. It's also the way Mum and Dad usually like to wake me up in the mornings, calling for me to help with chores.

The main control is in the kitchen and it looks like a kind of typewriter, but instead of the keys having letters on them, each one connects you to a different room of the hotel.

Yep! It's that simple. All you have to do is click the button you want, then speak into the trumpet-shaped mouthpiece and away you go.

Natter … natter … natter … natter … natter!

'I don't believe this,' Dad wheezed, looking like he was somewhere between laughing and crying. 'Maudlin, are you telling me that we can actually call Abraham?'

'I am!' the leprechaun chuckled.

'Just like that?' Mum gasped.

**JUST LIKE THAT!'** Maudlin replied. 'These handy gizmos connect you straight to the other side in a jiffy. I had one back when I was a lumpling and used to chat to my Aunt Influenza for hours. It's as easy as stomping on stinkbugs! All we have to do is—'

Without a moment's thought, she raised her arm above her head and then jammed the skell-a-phone key right into the middle of all the little round buttons on the yell-a-phone. There was a crunch and a squeal as the keys for the harpiery and the mud spa were bent aside, and then a tiny clicking noise as the skull shaped gadget snapped into place.

'There!' Maloney said, then folded her arms triumphantly. 'Got it first time!'

'So…' Nancy placed two of her hands on my shoulders from behind and leaned over us. 'What now?'

'Now – ' Maudlin whispered for dramatic effect. I could tell she was enjoying this – 'we press it. Frankie, would you like to do the honours?'

I jolted with surprise and felt a swooshy mixture of happiness and fear in my belly. I would never have imagined in a squillion years that I'd be making a phone call to my great-great-great-grandad's ghost when I got up this morning.

'Yes, go for it, my wee lamb,' Nancy encouraged me. 'Give it a tap!'

I looked at Mum and Dad and they both nodded. Then, trying mega-hard to stop my fingers from trembling, I lifted my hand and clicked the skell-a-phone key.

## A FAMILY REUNION

We all held our breaths and listened as the skell-a-phone line started crackling.

Even Granny Regurgita stopped shovelling termite trifle into her mouth and gawped.

At first there was nothing but the sound of rushing wind and a kind of distant wailing, until

**'Helloooooooooooooooooooooooooo?'** a faint and feeble voice suddenly echoed from the trumpet-shaped thingy that stuck out of the machine. It sounded ghostly and full of sadness. **'Helloooooooooooooooooooooooo?'**

All the hairs on the back of my neck prickled and my arms shivered with goosebumps.

'It's a ghoulie! Talk to it, boy!' Maloney barked at

me. 'Let it know we're here!'

'Ummm … Can you hear me?' I spoke into the mouthpiece. 'We want to talk to—'

**'Whoooooooo'stheeeeeeeeeeeerrrrrreeeeeeee?'** the echoey voice replied, louder than before.

'It's Fra—'

**'BEVERLY, IS THAT YOU? BEVERLY SNIPEGRASS?'** the voice interrupted. **'THANK GOODNESS!'**

'Erm … no … it's not Bev—'

**'WHERE HAVE YOU BEEN, BEVERLY? I'VE BEEN WAITING BLUNKING AGES! NEARLY SIXTY YEARS!'**

'My name is Frankie Banister!' I shouted. 'Can you hear me?'

**'WHO?'** the ghost-voice asked. **'WHAT HAVE YOU DONE WITH BEVERLY?'**

'Beverly's not here!'

**'WHERE DID SHE GO?'**

'I don't know,' I said, glaring at Maudlin for help. 'We're trying to reach Abraham Banister.'

**'NO, NOT ABRAHAM BANISTER! ARE YOU EVEN LISTENING? I'M LOOKING FOR BEVERLY SNIPEGRASS!'**

'That's enough of that, the wisp-witted eejit!' Maloney jabbed her finger at the skell-a-phone key and clicked it up and down several times. 'Let's try again, shall we?'

She released the button and we waited again as the sound of crackling drifted from the machine.

'Talk, Frankie,' Maudlin said to me with a wink. 'It helps the connection.'

I looked into the metal trumpet and tried to imagine my great-great-great-grandad listening on the other end.

'Hello?' I said. 'We want to speak with Abraham Banister. Are you there?'

We waited…

Nothing…

Nothing…

Nothing…

'Abraham Banister?' Maudlin joined in with me. 'Get to the phone, you flutter-brained fool.'

I leaned towards the machine and was about to speak again, when a cheerful sounding voice laughed on the other end of the line.

'Good gracicles!' it said. 'I wasn't expecting a chattywag at this hour!'

I swear to you, my reader friend, I don't know how I didn't fall over with astonishment at that moment. Was I actually talking to Great-Great-Great-Grandad Abraham?

'Abe, you old goat!' Maudlin hooted into the yell-a-phone. 'Is that you?'

'The very same!' he replied.

'It's Maudlin Maloney here. Remember me? We met when we were both holidaying in Antrim, giant-watching out on the causeway. I borrowed your binoculars, so I did.'

'Boogle my bunions! It can't be!' Abraham said. His voice was warm and friendly-sounding.

'It is, my friend, it is!' Maudlin croaked. She seemed just as excited as I was.

'How lovely to hear from you, Miss Maloney. How can I help you?'

'Well, I've actually got a few people here who'd like to say a skwinkly little hello.'

'You do?' Abraham chuckled. 'Who might that be?'

'There's your great-great-great-grandson, Frankie Banister,' the leprechaun beamed.

'Well, I never!' Abraham laughed.

**'HELLO, GRANDAD ABE!'** I yelled far too loudly into the metal trumpet.

'Good evening, my lad,' Abe said. 'You kept the family name? What a marvellous treat!'

'Nancy's here,' Maudlin continued.

**'HELLO, POPPET!'** our spider-chef called, dabbing a handkerchief to the corner of one of her eyes. I sometimes forget that Nancy actually knew Abe when he was alive.

'Then there's Frankie's parents, Rani and Bargeous,' Maudlin went on, but Mum and Dad were both completely overwhelped and barely managed a quick sobbed response. 'And Regurgita's here too!'

We all heard Grandad Abe gasp.

'My schmoopsy-poo?' he wheezed. 'My barnacled beauty? **HOW ARE YOU, MY DARLING?'**

Granny, who was halfway through emptying a huge bowl of whipped armadillo mousse down her gullet, turned and grunted at us as great blobs of the stuff trickled down her chin.

**'OH, BOG OFF!'** she bellowed. **'I HAD ENOUGH OF YOU THE FIRST TIME ROUND!'**

'Ah ha! There's the beauty-tooty I know and love!' Abe said with a sigh. 'I wish you could be here, my honey-blossom. Would you believe I'm at a deathly dinner party as we speak, with my good friends, Charles Dickens and Boudicca. It's a hoot! We were about to enjoy our dearly-departed desserts, but this is way more fun!'

'Now, Abe, hang on a moment...' Maudlin interrupted. 'I'd love to say this is just a cheery-chatty call, but we have some blunking big questions that need answering.'

'Oh?'

'You wouldn't believe the rumpskallious mess that's been occurinating at the hotel, so you wouldn't.'

'Oh, dear!' Abe's voice replied. 'My wonderful hotel! I do hope nothing dreadful has happened to her?'

'It's fine, Grandad Abe! The hotel is still in one piece, but we've had a right pickle with...' I don't know why I paused. 'With...'

'With what?' Abe pleaded. 'Don't leave an old ghost in suspense!'

'We've had a right pickle with your son,' I said, feeling that strange gurgly feeling in my belly again.

'With ... Oculus Nocturne!'

## A GHAST FROM THE PAST

Suddenly a ferocious blast of ice-cold wind erupted from behind us, knocking me against the yell-a-phone. I spun around just in time to see Mum and Dad sprawling across the kitchen floor and Maudlin flailing into the corner, narrowly missing the open door to the cellar. Nancy grabbed hold of the stove-front and held on tight, glancing around the room in panic.

In an instant, all the candles on the cake and dotted about the room went out, and I watched in dismay as the shadows swelled, filling the room with an enchanted darkness that even magicals couldn't see through.

'What's going on?' Granny bellowed from her

place at the table, but before anyone could utter a reply, lightning streaked across the ceiling and zig-zagged down the walls.

'Frankie!' I heard Mum yell, but I couldn't see where she was.

'We need to get out!' Maudlin cried next. 'Something's gone terribly wrong!'

Another blast of frosty wind stung my face and hands, and the air was filled with the deafening roar of howling ghostly voices and birds squawking. **'WHAT HAVE YOU DONE, LEPRECHAUN?!'** Granny roared.

**'I DON'T KNOW!'** Maloney shrieked. **'GET OUTTA HERE! I THINK WE'VE CONJURED SOMETHING FROM THE OTHER WORLD!'**

I tried to run to where I thought the kitchen door was, but my feet seemed to be frozen to the ground and I shivered uncontrollably as more and more gusts of blisteringly cold air toppled chairs and smashed plates in the blackness.

**'LOOK!'** It was Nancy's voice.

I twisted my head and caught sight of a brilliant

twinkle of green light that sparked into view on the opposite side of the room. Its dazzling glow shimmered and flickered, and I could just make out my mum and dad huddled together with Nancy as it glistened.

Then…

Without any warning, the glowing orb…blinked! My breath felt like it had been squeezed out of my lungs as I realised I was looking at a single green eyeball, burning in the darkness.

It glared around the room, then stopped and fixed its gaze on me.

'P-p-please don't hurt us,' I stammered, my skin prickling with horror.

It blinked again then changed colour as a second one appeared next to it. Suddenly I was looking into a pair of deep blue eyes.

'Hurt you?' a voice chuckled in the gloom. 'HA! What fun and nonsense!'

My whole body jolted with a mixture of alarm and relief, and I quickly felt the urge to burst into tears. The voice was kind and pleasant sounding, just like … **GRANDAD ABE!**

Slowly, more twinkling lights started to flicker in

the shadows, and… I wasn't sure, but as they glimmered, I thought I could make out the faint shape of a human figure standing there, next to the table. Its outline glistened delicately as the light spread around it like smoke … and … maybe I was going bonkers, but I swear it was waving!

'G… G… Grandad?'

'Good evening, young chap!' the thing in the dark replied with a laugh. 'It's me!'

'Abraham?' Maudlin grunted. 'What are you doing here? It was only supposed to be a skell-a-phone call.'

'You scared me halfway to Timbukthree!' Nancy heaved, clutching her four hands to her chest.

'Ha ha! Surprise!' My great-great-great-grandad shone into full view as the enchanted darkness filling the room returned to the regular kind. 'Goodness, look at your faces. Anyone would think you'd seen a ghost!'

I goggled in shock at the elderly spook with his bald head and curly moustache.

'Ah, it feels simply terrific to be back,' he beamed. 'Honkhumptious! It's like I never left!'

With that, he turned to where Granny Regurgita was gawping with the face of someone who'd just swallowed a wasps' nest.

'There's my schmoopsy-poo,' he tittered, holding out his arms for a hug. 'How about a little smooch?'

## CURIOUS GUESTS

'BLLLLAAAAAAAAAAAAAAAAAAAAAAA
AGGGGGGGGGHH HHHHH!'

Granny Regurgita smashed straight through the kitchen door, taking half the wall with it.

The last thing we saw was her massive silhouette sprinting like a bull with bellyache towards reception and a cloud of cement and brick dust swirling around her.

'BLLLLAAAAAAAAAAAAAAAAAAAAAAA
AGGGGGGGGGHH HHHHH!'

'Hmmm … that was a little unexpected,' Abraham stammered after a moment of silence. He looked at us with a mixture of bewilderment and amusement. Like this was something Granny did quite regularly

back when he was alive. 'Do you think we should pursue?'

By the time we'd hurried to the foyer and turned the corner under the archway, rumours and whispers had spread from room to room, and every customer staying with us was now bustling about in the reception hall, gossiping and asking questions.

Granny had torn through the crowd, scattering guests left and right, and was hiding behind my Great-Great-Aunt Zennifer's statue, peeking out like a kiddling playing hide-and-seek.

**'BOG OFF AND DON'T EVER COME BACK!'** she bellowed when she spotted us entering reception. **'I MEAN IT!'**

'Oh, goodness!' Mum said as we walked further into the enormous room and a sea of nosy faces with wide-eyed expressions turned to greet us. 'Evening!'

**'DON'T COME NEAR ME!'** Regurgita wailed, making the guests chatter excitedly. **'I'LL BLURGLE IF HE TRIES ANYTHING SMOOCHERISH!'**

I still felt dizzy with surprise at who had just

appeared in our kitchen, but I already knew I wasn't going to let my howling hippopotamus of a granny ruin this moment. How often do you get to meet a great-great-great-relative after all?

'Hello, everyone!' Dad said, smiling excitedly from beneath the archway.

'Never mind all your hello-ing, Mr Banister!' Madame McCreedie, the banshee, croaked from the middle of the crowd. She licked her crusty lips hungrily. 'Hurry now! The wallpaper's been whispering about a new arrival. What's here and is it edible?'

'Is it disgusterous?' shouted an over-excited impolump, his trunk-nose twitching this way and that.

'Wath it a denthitht?' called the Molar Sisters (triplet tooth fairies with extremely bad teeth, named Dentina, Gingiva and Fluora) in unison. 'Pleath thay it wath! We could uthe a good dentitht jutht now!'

'No, it was none of those things,' Dad said, grinning. He looked like he was about to start jumping up and down with delight at who had arrived. 'It was—'

Suddenly an explosion of ectoplasm erupted over a family of unsuspecting hinkapoots as Prince Grogbah appeared, clapping his tiny hands with glee and waggling his curly-toed feet.

'Oh, lummy!' he cooed, looking about the foyer. 'What's arrived? Is it something bitey?'

'Go away, Grogbog!' I grunted at the little ghost, before sticking out my tongue.

**'ZIP IT, SCUZZLING!'** he barked, raising his hand to silence me. 'I want to see the new guest. I do hope it's something dreaderous! Maybe today will be the day I'll see Frankie Banister get slobber-chomped!'

'Oh, get out of here, you wee jobby!' Nancy yelled, shaking her fists at the spoiled goblin prince. 'Don't you talk about Frankie like that!'

Ever since my great-great-uncle was defeated and carted off to the Himalayas, Grogbah has been haunting me non-stop. It's a nightmare! He almost never leaves my side, except when he waddles off for the occasional naked dip in the fountain (which he still insists is his own private plunge pool), and the rottly toad especially loves annoying me whenever he gets the chance. It's his way of getting revenge after being grunched-up in the garden, I suppose.

'Now is not the time!' Mum snapped, grabbing a broom from Ooof, the hotel's handyogre. She waved it towards the prince like he was a bad smell. 'Don't think I won't waft you away!'

'Shut your mumble-holes, all of you!' Grogbah shouted. 'I want to park my peepers on what's here! The wallpaper's been chattywagging about something terrorfumbling! A real creepsy cruminal. Whatever it is, it must be horribump!'

'Errm, no,' Mum replied, betraying a worried look for a moment. 'It's nothing … I mean … no one like that. The wallpaper is wrong.'

'It's never usually wrong!' Madam McCreedie rasped.

'It could be a boy-eating-borkle, perhaps?' Grogbah chuckled. 'Or a razor-toothed nifflehog?'

The guests crowding reception and the great spiral staircase gasped in alarm.

'Or a gristle-witch?' Prince Grogbah continued. 'Oh, yes! A nasty bone-stealing gurnip of a gristle-witch.'

'That's enough, you rambunking pook!' Maudlin Maloney's voice croaked from somewhere in the throng of magical guests. She was far too short to be seen among them all, and I never would have spotted her if she hadn't suddenly raised the nozzle of the vacuum cleaner into the air. 'You stop scaring everyone with your pint-sized prattle or I'll switch this on and you'll be guzzled a second time!'

Not even Prince Grogbah was stupid enough to argue with the ancient leprechaun. He scowled down to where Maloney was standing in the crowd, then glowered over at me.

'See you in your room, snotling!' he scoffed. 'I'm going to practise my opera singing all night long!'

With that, he vanished in another little explosion of ectoplasm, leaving our guests to gawk about with wide eyes.

In an instant the massive room was filled with the babble of questioning guests again as they shouted and called for answers.

'**GET OUT OF THE WAY!**' Maudlin Maloney pushed through the jostling mob. She reached Mum and me beside the stone reception counter then clambered up onto its surface. '**SHUT YOUR GABBLING GOBLETS IF YOU WANT TO FIND OUT WHO'S ARRIVED!**'

Everyone went silent. I looked up at Mum, and she nodded to me.

'Go on, darling,' she said with a wink and nudged me up onto the stone counter next to Maudlin. 'You can tell them.'

'Well,' I announced in my loudest voice. 'It's—'

'A stink demon?' called Mrs Venus from her wheelbarrow.

'A tusk-billed plunktipus?' shouted Horatio Croakum, the hotel's gardener.

'My Aunt Trudy?' wailed Berol Dunch, the geriatric mermaid, from the pool at the base of the fountain.

'NO! NONE OF THEM!' I yelled. If I didn't tell them now, our guests would never let me get the words out. 'IT WAS ... IT WAS ... IT WAS GREAT-GREAT-GREAT-GRANDAD ABRAHAM!'

## PANDEMONIUM

As I shouted the words, Dad stepped out from his spot under the archway, revealing the ghost of our long-dead relative, floating just behind him.

'Hello, there!' Grandad Abe smiled shyly and gave a little wave to everyone. 'Surprise!'

In seconds, the whole of reception was clamouring with raised voices.

'Is it really you?' gasped an elderly pine dryad.

**'I DON'T BELIEVE IT!'** hooted Reginald Blink, the cyclops.

'It can't be Abe … he had more skin the last time I saw him!' Berol Dunch insisted.

But it was! I found I couldn't help staring at the

elderly spook with his odd socks and twinkling blue eyes, as he nodded and smiled. I'd seen the painted portrait of my great-great-great-grandad every day of my life, and now I had a chance to finally get to know him. This should have been better than a million Trogmanay gifts all rolled into one! Although…

I wasn't sure why, but that old familiar feeling of doubt bubbled in my belly again. Just because Abe was here and seemed friendly enough, it didn't mean that all the terrible things Oculus had told us weren't true. What was it Grogbah had said about the wallpaper's gossiping? Something terrorfumbling? A real cruminal?

'Ere! Whath all thith we've heard about you being a thneaky tho-and-tho?' the Molar Sister lisped in unison, as if they'd read my thoughts.

'A what?' the old ghost replied, looking slightly shocked.

'We heard you're a grim-hearted gurnip!' gurgled an elderly anemononk.

'A right **RUMPSCALLION!**' Reginald Blink

joined in.

'Good gracicles! No!' Abe gasped. 'You've been misinformed!'

'Then what about your blunkerly son?' Lady Leonora, scoffed as she materialised in mid-air.

'That little whippersnooper necromanicled me and made me act as a ... a ... COMMON SERVANT!!'

'I NEARLY DIED!' wailed Wailing Norris from halfway up the spiral staircase.

'You're already dead, you cretinous idiot!' Lady Leonora snapped at the trembling, wild-haired spook. Then she turned her attention back to Abe. 'But, still…'

'I can't be blamed for what that boy got up to! I can't even remember him. Not really! It's not my fault if he tried to destroy the hotel!'

'I don't think we told you that,' Maudlin said, raising an eyebrow and scowling at the moustachioed ghost.

'What?' Abe chuckled. 'No … I just sensed it!'

'You sensed it?' Maudlin asked.

'Indeed!' Grandad Abe tittered. 'Something us spirits are skilled at. Isn't that right, Lady Leonora?'

'Ghosts are terribly intelligent,' Leonora agreed, nodding pompously. 'I myself am particularly astute!'

'Have you two met before?' Maudlin grunted, looking sceptical. 'How do you know Lady Leonora's name?'

'It's a ghost thing!' Abe said. 'Our magical minds, know more than most...'

'Charmed, I'm sure!' Lady Leonora gasped at the compliment and giggled annoyingly.

Maloney opened up her mouth to speak again, but Leonora plucked a wispy fan out of the air and waved it at the ancient leprechaun.

'Shoo!' the ghost hissed as she floated down to the ground. 'The master of the house will not be wanting to spend another moment with the likes of you.'

'What makes you think he wants to see your mangy mug?!' Maudlin hissed back, but the haughty grey ghost ignored her.

'Come, my dear,' Lady Leonora warbled at Abe.

'Now that you're one of us, you'll be wanting to learn of all the best haunts around the hotel. I know a marvellous spot on the seventh floor that's perfect for practising your screams!'

With that, the lady-ghost went to link her arm around Grandad Abe's and ... he shrieked!

**'DON'T TOUCH ME!'** he bellowed, recoiling from the mortified-looking ghost.

'HOW RUDE!' Leonora squawked. She was so surprised that she exploded a tiny burp of ectoplasm onto the floor tiles.

Silence suddenly filled the busy room again as everyone gawped at Abe.

The old ghost glared at us all, then grinned nervously.

'I ... I do beg your pardon,' he mumbled. If ghosts were capable of blushing, I think his entire body would have turned red as a tomato at that moment.

'I'm ... ummm ... I'm terribly tired. Travelling from the Land of the Dead is an exhausting journey! I'm a married fellow and if it's all the same to you,

I'd just like to spend a spot of snuggle-time with my darling wife.'

Everyone turned to look at Granny Regurgita, who was in the middle of trying to tiptoe up the first flight of the staircase. She stopped and grimaced.

## 'NOT ON YOUR NELLY!'

'But, schmoopsy-poo!' Abraham begged. 'I've come all this way!'

'Ooooh, it'th tho romantic,' the Molar Sisters sighed in unison. 'I hope they kith, all thlobbery-like!'

Granny's cheeks suddenly puffed out and I thought she was going to be sick.

'Don't even think about it, you grimblish old creep!' my grizzly granny bellowed. 'I had a go at being wifely and lovelicious the first time round and I thought it was **GUT-HONKING!** I'd rather snuggle with a sabre-toothed snuzzbungle than spend more time with you!'

And that was it...

Granny galumphed up the great staircase like a

demented rhinoceros and vanished out of sight.

'Oh, bother!' Grandad Abe mumbled miserably.

Glancing over at the elderly ghost, the doubt in my head began to melt away. He looked so sad, just floating there, and I couldn't help feeling sorry for him.

I was about to call his name, but the clamour of our nosy guests instantly drowned me out as they grabbed their chance and started yelling and hollering questions again.

'What can you remember about Oculus?'

'Almost nothing,' Abe whimpered. 'I've been a ghost for nearly a hundred years! I can't even recall what he looked like!'

'What's it like to pop your clonkers?'

**'COLD!'** Abe cried.

'Why did you run away and abandon your first son and wife?'

'I didn't!' Abe cringed. 'I can't remember them, I truly can't! It's all just one big smudgy blur!'

Guests crowded around the startled ghost, while more and more appeared on the balconies, drawn by all the noise.

Abe's reappearance had split the hotel's inhabitants into two teams. Some were cheering and celebrating his return while others were shouting and waving their fists in the air, obviously still not sure Abe should be welcomed as a hero if the rumours were true.

It was chaos! Mum, Dad and Nancy were doing their best to control the situation, but a bit of juicy gossip was far more important than good behaviour to most magicals.

Guests were whooping and yelling, and Berol Dunch even threw the remains of a sardine she'd been chewing on!

I watched as if the world had turned to slow motion as the disgusting thing sailed through the air, passed straight through Abe's head and hit the wall with a squidgy splat.

'Take that!'

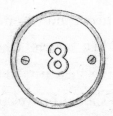

## DON'T MESS WITH MAUDLIN MALONEY

## 'BREAK IT UP!!!!!'

The cracked voice squawked so loudly, everyone (including Abe) stopped what they were doing and goggled about with surprise.

I turned to look at Maudlin as she growled on the reception counter next to me. She fumbled with something on her belt then raised her arm into the air.

## 'STOP YOUR MADNESS!!'

Between her gnarled fingers the ancient leprechaun was clutching a small bottle made from blue glass.

## 'I THINK THAT'S QUITE ENOUGH, YOU PACK OF HOODLUMPS!' she bellowed.

# 'GET BACK TO YOUR ROOMS!'

With that, the grizzled bad luck fairy hurled the little bottle at the black and white tiled floor with a grunt. It shattered in a cloud of sickly yellow smoke and instantly the room was filled with a curious popping sound, like when you pour badger milk on puffed-maggot breakfast cereal.

For the teensiest of seconds nothing happened, and then…

## 'AAAAAAAAAEEEEEEEEEEGGGGHH HHHHH!!'

All at once, every single angry guest filling the foyer or bustling their way towards us lurched straight off the ground and started flying backwards at breakneck speed, as if they were being pulled by the elastic at the rear of their underpants.

**'WHAT'TH GOIN' ON!?'** the Molar Sister's yelped as they whizzed past, nearly knocking me off my feet.

## 'AAAAAEEEEE!'

Guests zoomed around the staircase and hurtled between the chandeliers. A gaggle of potato-sized dust pooks rolled the wrong way up the banister and Berol Dunch was dragged out of the fountain and down the corridor towards the swimming pool by her tail, leaving a wet trail on the floor as she went.

**'PUT ME DOWN!'**

I watched in amazement as bodies tumbled through the air until, one by one, they all vanished down the many hallways that led away from the great spiral staircase on all ten floors, followed by the sound of hundreds of slamming bedroom doors.

In ten seconds flat, me, Mum and Dad, Nancy and Maudlin were alone with Grandad Abe in the middle of the deserted foyer.

There was a moment of confused gawking until Nancy let out a great big grunt.

A grumpling who'd been watching the whole drama unfold from next to the reception desk had accidentally zoomed straight through Nancy's bluish/purple hairdo as he was magically launched off the floor. Now, our unfortunate spider-chef's curls were sticking out in all directions like a well-shampooed palm tree. Her tartan hat was drooped over one eye, and her glasses had been flung off altogether. She looked like she'd just been dragged through a tornado backwards.

'Oooch, I say!' she huffed. 'My perm! I've only just had this done! A wee bit of warning would have been nice, Maudlin, If I'd been one step further to the left, that poor grumpling would have taken my head off!' She fumbled for her spectacles on the

floor, found them and placed them back on her nose, blinking all eight of her eyes. 'What in the blunkers was that, anyway?'

Maudlin grinned a crooked grin.

'That was a **STOP ALL YOUR NONSENSE** charm,' she chuckled. 'Stole the recipe from a bogrunt back in Tipperary years ago, and I've been perfecting it ever since. Very handy, I'd say.'

'Indeed!' Grandad Abe mumbled, looking at

Maloney with a mixture of fear and gratitude. 'I thank you kindly. You always know just the right charm.'

'Think nothing of it!' the leprechaun croaked. 'Though it won't keep those ruffians and rumpers in their rooms for long. I'd say it's about time we all got ourselves to bed-i-bunks.'

Nobody said anything. It was way past midnight, but everyone was far too excited to head off to their rooms.

'There's going to be a lot of explaining to do tomorrow, whether you like it or not, Abe.'

'Oh … yes. I suppose there will be.'

'Honestly, my old friend!' Maudlin half-scolded, half-chuckled. 'Who shows up uninvited to a gaggle of gossipy grahams at a time like this? You're a glutton for trouble, so you are!'

'I just wanted to visit after talking to you all. Oh, bother and blast it! I should never have come. Everyone thinks I'm a skuzzler!'

'Well, I never believed any of the rumours, Abraham!' Dad said. 'I don't think you're a skuzzler and I'm glad you're here.'

'Me too!' Mum added.

'There'll be plenty of time for that stuff tomorrow,' Maudlin said. 'Abe, you can sleep on my caravan steps, where I can keep an eye on you. The rest of you … **GET TO BED!'**

We had a billion things we wanted to ask my great-great-great-grandad, but nobody was brave enough to argue with Maudlin Maloney.

**'GO!'**

## THE FOURTH KEYHOLE

The second the sun was up, I was dressed and rattling down through the floor of my bedroom in my **BRILLIANT** chair-lift quicker than I'd ever done before.

Grogbah had kept true to his word and had sat spinning on my model-globe, singing at the top of his voice all night, so morning couldn't have come fast enough.

Today was Abe's actual one hundred and seventy-fifth birthday and I couldn't wait to spend the day with him. There was SO much I wanted to know about his travels and adventures.

Whatever doubts I'd had yesterday were gone and a buzz of excitement fizzed in my brain. I couldn't believe I'd let stupid Prince Grogbah make me feel nervous!

I reached the library floor with a *BUMP* and darted over to the doors that led through to reception.

'Grandad Abe!' I shouted as I flung the doors wide, then nearly fell over backwards when I saw the foyer was already filled with hundreds of guests. I guess I wasn't that much of an early bird, after all.

'Frankie, my dear!' Nancy called from the stone counter. 'Over here!'

I glanced across the enormous room and saw my family gathered there, and they too were gawping at my great-great-great-grandad.

'It was right here!' I heard Abe say as he was floating in circles around the stone reception desk, with a look of frustration on his face.

'There are only three keyholes, Abe,' Mum said. She reached inside her top and pulled out the brass key that hung around her neck on a chain. 'See? I should know – I'm in charge of them.'

'No, no, no – there definitely used to be four!'

Abe said. 'Fish, snake, bumblebee, octopus!'

'Morning, boy!' Maudlin grumbled when she spotted me. 'What time do you call this?'

Abe looked up and smiled.

'Good day to you, young chap!' he beamed, grinning a mischievous grin. 'You've arrived at precisely the right moment!'

'What's going on?' I asked, pushing my way to the front of the crowd.

'Well,' Mum interrupted. She stepped forward and raised her hands like she was about to deliver a speech. 'Last night, after you'd all gone to bed, Bargeous and I had a chat and we decided that we'd be bonkers not to throw our usual party for Abe's one hundred and seventy-fifth birthday. Especially now that he'd actually be attending this one.'

'And when we woke this morning and let Abe know about our idea…' Dad looked at Abe with glee. 'You tell them! Tell everyone what you told us!'

'Oh, righty ho,' Abe chuckled. He floated slightly higher so everyone could see him clearly. 'I said we simply must throw a big bash in the ballroom.'

I stopped and thought for a moment.

'But … we haven't got a ballroom,' I mumbled, wondering if being kept up all night by Grogbah had affected my concentration.

'THAT'S WHAT I SAID!' Dad blurted excitedly.

'Ah, well, I'm afraid you're both wrong,' Abe smiled. 'I think you'll find we do. It's **SPLENDIFEROUS!'**

'Where is it, my wee lamb?' Nancy asked. 'I've never heard of it.'

'Ha ha! You'll see, Nancy,' Abe laughed. 'I just need to locate this elusive octopus lock. I know it's on the reception counter somewhere!'

Octopus lock? I'd never seen that one before and I knew the desk like the back of my hand.

I looked at the keyholes on the front of the stone block and checked them for myself. Everything was just like it had always been. The three slots were encircled by different gold symbols and each one worked an entrance to the hotel.

If you turned the key in the fish lock, Aunt

Zennifer's fountain at the centre of the room slid away to reveal the sea door, a deep well that stretched below the building and out to the ocean. That entrance was mostly used by mermaids, anemenonks, swelkies and kulpies.

The snake keyhole opened and closed the front door to the street.

The bumblebee unlocked the sky door, high up in the dome of reception.

I'd seen Mum operate them a squillion times, and I knew for certain that she was right. There was definitely no octopus symbol.

'Are you sure you're not just a bit hazy, deary?' said Nancy.

'Not at all! I remember it perfectly!' Abe glared at the stone desk and stroked his moustache. 'We used it all the time. It operated the elevator to…'

The ghost's voice hushed to an almost silent muttering.

'I think it might be time to get you back to a staircase for more rest. Ooof's cellar steps are free, I'm sure he won't mind,' Nancy continued. 'You must still be exhausted from your journey, Abe. Does that sound goo—'

**'I'VE GOT IT!'** Abe blurted, stopping Nancy in her tracks.

'What? What have you got?' Maudlin asked.

'Water! We need sea water!' Grandad Abe clapped his ghostly hands together and wisped quickly around the corner of the desk towards us. 'It's all coming back! We had to put an enchantment on the keyhole after an infestation of rumpuswumps got in and practically wrecked the ballroom with their wild partying'

We all looked at each other, not quite sure what to do.

'I haven't finished my tea. Will this do?' Dad said, holding up his mug.

'No good!' Grandad Abe replied. 'It needs to be salt water.'

'But I'm drinking shrimp-scale tea,' Dad said. 'It's salty as a sardine's spittle!'

**'MARVELLOUS!'** Grandad Abe barked. 'In that case… Here, Bargeous – pour it over the top of

the desk.'

I glanced at Mum, who was busily nodding her approval at Dad. She looked so excited, I half-expected to see her head floating off her shoulders.

'You watch this,' Abe beamed. 'It's terrific! Quickly, now!'

Dad lifted his mug above the counter and poured what was left of the shrimp-scale tea over its surface. Then we waited as the pinky-red drink spread over the cold grey block, and...

'**LOOK!**' Mum gasped.

The hairs on the back of my neck prickled and my pointy ears twitched, as the top of the desk rippled and swirled like the stone itself had turned to liquid. From a point right in the middle of the countertop, eight gold tentacles emerged from the rock and spread outwards, wriggling and flexing their suckers until they reached its edges and started squirming down the sides towards the ground.

'It's unbelievable!' Dad wheezed. 'Tell me you're all seeing this!'

'We're seeing it all right, Bargeous!' Nancy said,

blinking her many eyes in amazement. 'Och, it's beautiful!'

Finally, just as the golden octopus tentacles reached the floor, there was a small creak of metal and a keyhole appeared right at their centre.

Nobody spoke.

We all stared with pounding hearts and gaping mouths.

'Well?' Grandad Abe finally said, breaking the silence. 'What are you waiting for, Rani? Give the key a try.'

'Go on,' said Dad, patting Mum on the shoulder.

'Here goes,' Mum said. 'Hold onto your bumly-bits.' She slowly lifted her trembling hand and inserted the key into the octopus lock. Then, with one swift movement, she turned it.

***CLUNK!***

## WELCOME UNDER

There was a violent judder beneath our feet and the ear-splitting sound of grinding gears.

Before we even realised what was happening, the stone counter and a large circular section of the black and white tiles started spinning and lowering down through the floor, taking us with it, and leaving our gobsmacked guests to stand and stare in surprise.

'Wimble my webs!' Nancy cried, grabbing hold of my arm with all four of her hands to steady herself. 'What in the worlds?'

'Ha ha! I knew it,' Grandad Abe laughed. 'You're all going to love this. Just you wait and see!'

I glanced at Mum and Dad, who were both

speechless with wonder as the elevator continued to rumble down into the ground, rotating as it went, like we were standing on top of some massive corkscrew, burrowing into the earth. All around us, gigantic cogs whirred and spun against the walls of the lift-shaft. How had we not known all of this was right beneath the foyer?

Deeper we went, sinking further and further below reception.

'How far does this contraption go?' Mum asked nervously.

'And what's at the bottom when we get there?' Maudlin added, pulling a mangy rabbit-foot charm from a pouch on her belt and rubbing it between her thumb and stumpy forefinger. 'All this spinny-jiggering is making me feel blurty, so it is!'

Grandad Abe smiled cheerfully at us. 'Nearly there,' he said. 'Don't you worry, Madam. It's all perfectly safe.'

'Madam?' Maudlin scoffed as she teetered about. 'You won't think me so madamly when I'm pukey-pootling all over the place.'

Just as the foyer was becoming a tiny point of light at the top of the deep shaft, there was a gust of dusty air and we emerged through the ceiling of a large room.

'Oh, good grumptious!' Maudlin gasped, instantly forgetting she was feeling sick as we rattled past a huge cobwebby chandelier. 'This place is ... what is it, exactly?'

The spinning platform made one last full turn and lowered to the floor with a sudden bump.

No one moved.

I swear to you, my human-reader-friend, I've never felt more excited in my life so far, as I did at that moment. The room ahead of us was like some kind of ... of ... train station!

'What the blunkers?' Dad mumbled to himself as he stepped off the lift and shuffled over to a nearby railing to get a better look.

'Good, isn't it?' said Grandad Abe.

Me and Mum ran to join Dad at the railing and we all stood there gawping at the bizarre room spreading out before us.

We'd stopped on a raised veranda with two small staircases curving down on either side to what looked like a wooden station platform below. Dotted along the walkway were lampposts like the ones on Brighton Promenade, and each one had a tatty flag hanging from it with the words, '**WELCOME UNDER**' stitched across them. Further down the platform stood a wonky snack-cart, advertising '**POPPED CORNS AND CALLUSES**' and '**CANDIED CARBUNKLES**'. Beyond that was a cobwebby old ticket kiosk with a large sign above its cracked window. The writing on the sign was painted in red and yellow lettering – you know, the old-fashioned kind, all curly and twisty – and despite being covered in a blanket of dust, I could easily read it:

*The Briny Ballroom and Pleasure Gardens*
*Admittance: One Shilling*

'The Briny Ballroom?' Mum half-gasped, half-wheezed.

'Pleasure Gardens?' I joined in. I liked the sound of those. Nancy had once taken me on a day trip while she was wearing one of her glimmers (a special kind of spell that made her appear like a human granny in public) to a town further up the coast. We visited the pleasure gardens there, and they had games and amusements and a noisy band playing all day. It was **FANTASTIC!**

'Wait till you see it!' Grandad Abe chuckled at us. He was suddenly beaming with excitement.

'But...' Nancy said. 'Why didn't I know about this place? I've worked at the hotel since it opened. There's no way I couldn't have seen it!'

'Hmmm ... sounds suspicious,' Maudlin interrupted. She grabbed what looked like a small magnifying glass from one of her pockets and ogled at the giant spider through it. 'Let me take a look at you for a winksy second.'

'Err, what are you doing?' said Nancy.

'This here is a swizzlescope,' Maudlin replied, still peering through the little lens. 'It can spot bamboozlements from a mile off, and … ho, ho, you've got one on ya! A bigg'un!'

'What?'

Maudlin fetched another small bottle from her belt and handed it to Nancy.

'Drink this! There's a pinch of disrememberment going on here.'

'What is it?' Nancy asked nervously.

'The tears of a fib fairy,' Maudlin whispered dramatically. 'Great for removing bamboozlements.'

We all watched as Nancy pulled a face. She looked uncomfortably at the greenish liquid inside then raised the tiny bottle to her lips and swigged it.

'Tastes like liquorice!' Maudlin cackled.

'Well?' Mum said after a moment. 'Anything?'

'Oh!!' Nancy suddenly clutched her hands to her chest. 'Agh! Of course I knew about it! I loved the Briny Ballroom!'

'What did I tell you?' Maudlin cooed with a proud look. 'Manky Old Maloney can sort out ya' problems, so she can.'

'That's powerful stuff!' Nancy laughed. 'It's all coming back like a bolt from beyond. Regurgita's the reason I don't remember it any more.'

'Sadly, my darling was never much of a fan of water, was she?' Abe joined in.

'She's certainly not keen on washing,' Dad said, 'but I don't understand what that has to do with anything.'

'Regurgita always threatened that if Abe popped his clonkers and left her to manage the business alone, she'd enchant this half of the hotel and make everyone forget about it,' Nancy continued, scratching her head. 'It looks like she kept her promise.'

'Are you telling me that Regurgita brain-burped

the lot of you?' Mum asked, looking appalled.

'I'm afraid it looks that way,' said Grandad Abe. 'I seem to recall my shmoopsy-poo hated coming down here because the under-the-sea part never really tickled her fancy.'

**'UNDER THE SEA?'** Maudlin yelped. **'THE OTHER HALF OF THE HOTEL IS UNDER THE SEA!?'**

Great-Great-Great-Grandad Abraham grinned another of his mischievous grins and floated over to a metal lever that was sticking up through the wooden platform near the ticket kiosk. It was nearly as tall as I was!

'Just wait,' he said.

With that, Abe held out his hands and wriggled his fingers at the lever. There was a sharp squeal of metal and the lever jolted sideways, followed by the high-pitched clickity-clack of rusted wheels travelling along a rickety rail.

## THE ATILANTUS

'Ooooh, it's coming!' Abe laughed, fidgeting with joy. 'I knew she would still work after all these years!' He pointed to an archway in one of the walls at the far side of the room. 'Watch! She'll be here soon!'

Speechless, I peered over the edge of the wooden platform and noticed there was a brass track running along the floor, like the kind you'd see on a fairground ride. I followed it with my eyes and felt a tingle of excitement whiz through me.

The track came out of the archway that Abe was pointing to, ran alongside the station, and then vanished back through a second arch on the other side of the room.

## CLATTER! SQUEAK! JANGLE! CLUNK!

'What's that noise?' Mum asked.

'Any second now,' Abe said, not really listening to Mum.

And he was right…

Just as Mum was about to ask more questions, there was a flash of light and a brilliantly-polished brass … thingy rattled into view.

I don't even know how to begin describing it. It was one of the most **TERRIFIC** things I've ever seen.

What rolled into the station looked like some kind of train-car in the shape of a giant fish skeleton. There were ribs of shiny metal all the way along it, and ornately-carved fins and a tail at the sides and back. Nestled inside were four rows of plump blue velvet seats, and where the eyes of the brass sea creature should be, burned two lanterns that sliced the dusty air with their bright green beams.

'Isn't she wonderful?' Grandad Abe chortled, when nobody made a sound.

'W…what is it?' Dad stammered. He **LOVES** gadgets and machines and stuff, so he was pulling a face like Hoggit, my pet pygmy soot-dragon, does when he's been a good boy and Mum lets him have the leftovers from our dinner.

'This, my dear friends and family, is the **ATILANTUS!'** Abe said with pride. 'I designed her myself. Constructed by a team of over five thousand highly-skilled mergullies, she was.'

'What's it for?' Maudlin Maloney croaked.

'She!' Abe corrected the ancient leprechaun, stroking the machine like its feelings had been hurt. 'The Atilantus is a she! And she's here to take you off on a voyage to the funnest, most

excellent, most **HONKHUMPTIOUS** place you could hope to visit this side of the Bermuda Triangle. **ALL ABOARD!!!'**

'I'm not getting in that thing!' Maudlin squawked. 'It looks leakish!' But before she had time to protest, Nancy had scooped the grumpy bad luck fairy up and bundled her into the fish-shaped carriage.

'Och, I cannae wait to see it again!'

In only a few moments we were all scrabbling between the contraption's ribs and chattering noisily. Nancy took the back seats all to herself, with

Maudlin wriggling about on the row in front of her. Mum and Dad took the next row of plush blue chairs, leaving the front for me and Grandad Abe.

'Does it go fast?' Mum said.

'How long will it take to get there?' Dad asked, shifting about impatiently. 'Will we see dolphins?'

'It's going to be grand! I was a whirly-girly back then in the Briny Ballroom!' Nancy cooed. She was gripping Maudlin by the shoulders to stop her from jumping back out.

'Leave me be!!' the grizzly leprechaun howled, but Nancy's four hands held her fast. 'I'm warning you, spider!'

'You'll thank me when we get there, my wee lamb!'

**'I'LL CURSE YOU WHEN WE GET THERE!!!'**
Maudlin hollered back.

## WHOOMMFF!!

'Go on, Frankie.'

I glanced up at Grandad Abe and saw he was looking at a shiny brass panel set into the front of the carriage. On it, there was a single button made of glass, right at its centre. It was large and circular, and it glowed the same colour as the beams that poured out of the fish's lantern-eyes.

'Push it! You're in the driver's seat.' Abe said with a wink.

I placed my hand on the button and watched as the light sliced up between my fingers, shimmering and dancing across our faces.

'Don't be nervous, my boy,' Grandad Abe smiled.

'It's wonderful down there under the sea!'

With his head facing towards me, I noticed Abe's left eye had turned green in the Atilantus's glow. For a split-second, the sight of it reminded me of Oculus and the hairs on the back of my neck prickled at the memory.

I opened my mouth to speak, when—

'WOO HOO!!!' Nancy, more excited than a gaggle of dust pooks who'd just got into the vacuum cleaner bag, reached across the rows of seats and placed her hand over mine. 'HERE WE GO! HOLD ON TO YOUR HUNKLES!'

The button clicked loudly and huge clouds of steam billowed out from either side of the bizarre machine.

We juddered on the spot for a moment, like the lid on a pan of boiling water. Then, before we even had a chance to shriek, the Atilantus rocketed forwards with an almighty WHOOMMFF and we hurtled towards the archway ahead of us.

Fusty stale air whipped and whistled through the metal ribs of our fish-shaped train as it careered out of the station room and plunged downwards, nose-diving into complete and utter darkness, clattering and squeaking with rust as it went.

Wind stung my eyes and I gripped the sides of

my seat so hard I thought my fingers were going to drop off. The lanterns at the front of the Atilantus only lit up a tiny section of the tracks ahead of us and they were a blur beneath its wheels.

'WE'RE GOING TO DIE!' It was Dad who screamed first, followed by Mum and Nancy … and … I'm not ashamed to say I was howling like a baby right along with them. The only voice I didn't hear as we tore through the blackness was Maudlin Maloney. I think the sudden **WHOOOSH** had stunned her into gobsmacked silence … **HA HA!**

'Isn't this top notch?' Grandad Abe yelled above the roar of rushing wind as we seemed to hit a bend in the track, then swooped sharply upwards through the dark again. 'Thrilling!'

**'THRILLING? YOU BLUNKING EEJIT!'** It looked like Maloney had finally found her voice. I glanced over my shoulder and caught sight of the petrified leprechaun in the green glow, wild-eyed with her ratty dreadlocks streaming out behind her like laundry that had been pegged out to dry in a hurricane. **'I WISH I'D NEVER SET**

ME PEEPERS ON THE LOT OF YOU,
SO HELP ME!'

'Almost out!' Abe half-shouted, half-laughed.
'Five... four ... three...'

'THE SPOOK'S GONE POTTY!' Maudlin
screamed. 'GET ME OFF THIS CONFOUNDED
CONTRAP—'

Suddenly, there was another **WHOOMMFF**
of steam and a squeal of the battered wheels, and we
burst into a brilliant blue light.

For the teensiest of seconds, I thought we'd
emerged above the ground – until I saw waves
crashing overhead and I realised we were **UNDER
THE SEA!**

The Atilantus was zooming through a sort of
clear tunnel like a fishy bullet from an ancient pistol.

'**THIS IS AMAZING!**' Mum cried as we
zipped among what looked like a sunken forest of
tree trunks. '**THE PIER!**'

She was right! Grandad Abe's invention had
exploded out from underground and was racing
between the hundreds of wooden legs that held up

Brighton Pier.

'I told you!' the old ghost chortled as we raced onwards.

We may have been flying along at break-neck speed, but I could clearly see the Atilantus was travelling inside a glass tube, held together with great clasps of rusty bronze and, from the looks of it, stretching away into the distance ... we had a long way to go. A **VERY** long way to go. So I sat back and did my best to enjoy the ride, trying not to think about the fact we were in an extremely old and decrepit machine, heading hundreds of metres beneath the ocean.

## OH, I DO LIKE TO BE BENEATH
## THE SEASIDE

For miles and miles, the Atilantus whistled onwards,
going deeper and deeper as we went.

Every now again we'd reach a rickety bend in the
tracks or come across a leak in the tunnel and get
soaked as the Atilantus exploded through the
curtain of water that rained down through it, but
mostly … well, mostly we just kept shooting straight
out into the open sea.

'It's getting a bit murky,' Dad said to Abe from
the second row. 'How far are we going?'

I turned and looked at him, and I could tell he
was starting to have the same worried thoughts as
me. We were getting very, very deep underwater,

and it was starting to get very, very dark on the other side of the glass.

'Not long!' Abe replied, smiling to himself. 'We should be seeing it any second … there!' He jabbed a ghostly finger at a large dark shape in the gloom outside.

'What is it?' I asked, squinting my eyes to

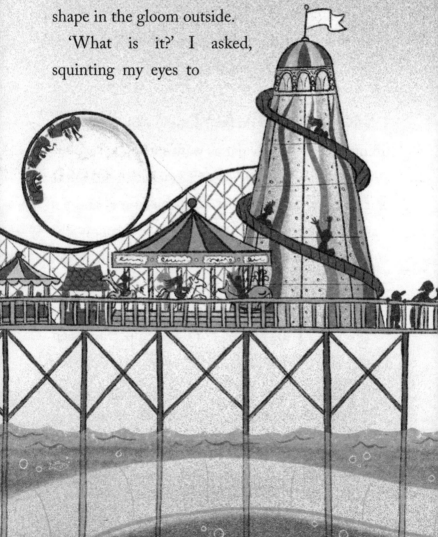

try and figure out what I was staring at. It looked like a colossal crack in the seabed.

'That, my dear boy, is the Banister-Bulch Trench! Discovered by me and your great-great-great-granny yonks ago!'

'It looks deep!' Mum squeaked nervously.

'Ooooh, it is,' Abe said. 'Very deep indeed.'

'And … are … we … going … down … there?' Mum asked.

**'MOST CERTAINLY!'** Grandad cooed as the glass tube reached the edge of the enormous gorge and we plunged downwards again. **'HOLD ON TIGHT! THIS IS THE BEST BIT!'**

Without any warning, the Atilantus began twisting and dipping, this way and that, like an out of control rollercoaster. In the light of the fish-eye lanterns, I watched with horror and excitement as we dived beneath crags of stone and zipped between the broken remains of old shipwrecks, glistening with treasure.

Over and under, around and through, we hurtled into the trench, zig-zagging wildly. Thundering between great rocky chimneys that spewed columns of volcanic ash, until ... suddenly, through the glass walls of the tunnel I caught sight of one of the most beautiful things I've **EVER** seen.

Everybody gasped as we started to slow down and we gawped at the view spreading out in front of us.

Nestled right into the bottom of the gargantuan gorge was a stupendous garden of the weirdest, most gigantic underwater plants you could imagine. It went on for miles!

'How is this all down here?' Mum asked.

'A visiting tiki-trog helped us out with a warm-your-welks charm years and years ago,' Abe replied with a smile. 'It might be in the freezing depths of the sea, but the Banister-Bulch Trench is a tropical oasis.'

Below, I could see honking great fans and domes of pink and gold coral, surrounded by a huge forest of billowing yellow kelp. A massive maze of anemones in every colour imaginable pulsated a little way off, and vast lawns of green and purple seagrass spread out, dancing in the currents … And all of it was glowing as brightly as the flowers in Mr Croakum's flowerbeds.

It almost looked like the Milky Way had sunk to the deepest depths of the ocean and we'd just found it, twinkling in the bottom of an immense trench!

'Would you look at that!' Nancy blurted.

'It's wonderful!' Mum joined. 'I … I can't believe it!'

But … that's not even the best bit, my reader friend, because right in the middle of the never-ending undersea shrubbery was **THE OTHER HALF OF THE HOTEL!!!**

## THE BRINY BALLROOM

'There it is!' Grandad Abe hooted. 'What a sight for spookery eyes.'

Nobody spoke.

All of us, including Manky Old Maloney, were flabbergusted and watched in silence as the tracks took one last swoop under an archway of fiery red coral and curved towards the building at the centre of the glowing pleasure gardens.

'The Briny Ballroom,' Abe chuckled. 'We've reached our destination.'

As we approached, I wasn't even sure what I was gawping at. The building was a kind of colossal clear orb, held in place on the seabed by huge claws of gleaming gold.

The Atilantus rattled around a final bend and passed through an opening into the base of the humongous glass ball.

I don't think there are enough words in the whole world to fully describe what we all saw as our fish-train chugged into the small arrivals station, just like the one below the hotel reception.

'This way,' Grandad Abe said as we came to a shaky stop. He floated past me, onto the wooden platform, then gestured for us to follow. Everyone clambered out through the metal ribs of the fish skeleton, eager to get a better look.

I swayed onto solid ground with knees like jelly, although I didn't care one little bit. I felt like someone had reached inside my head and scrambled my brains with an egg beater, but that wasn't going to stop me now! The shock of meeting my long-dead great-great-great-grandad yesterday was enough to make me think I was dreaming, but riding a mechanical fish skeleton into the depths of the ocean, and discovering a whole new part of the hotel **ALL BEFORE LUNCH** was verging on

**BONKERS** and **I LOVED IT!**

'Come on, darling,' Mum said to me, practically hopping with delight.

Ahead of us was a railing, just like the one in the 'Welcome Under' room, and I couldn't wait to reach it and get a better look at the cavernous place.

We all shuffled over to the balcony edge like we'd had few too many sips of bluebottle brandy, and…

**'CORRR!'** Maloney cooed as she doddered up next to me. She planted her stumpy hands on her hips and peered about with a grin on her face.

'What did I tell you, Maudlin?' Nancy said, her eight eyes bulging with surprise. She gave the little leprechaun a nudge with her nearest elbow. 'I said you'd thank me when we got here.'

Maloney didn't reply, she was too busy gawking, and I can't say I blame her. Everything Grandad Abe had said was true.

The Briny Ballroom was **HONKHUMPTIOUS!**

No … it was more than **HONKHUMPTIOUS!!**

It was **HUMDEFFEROUS!!!**

Before us, underneath the high walls and ceiling

of glass, stretched the most enormous circular dance floor I'd ever seen. It looked a bit like the floor of the hotel reception, with loads of patterned rings spiralling into the centre, but instead of black and white tiles, it was paved in thousands and thousands of tiny blue and purple seashells. Right in the middle, where Great-Great-Aunt Zennifer's fountain would have been if we were back at home, was an ornate tree carved out of silver.

Beyond the tree there was a bandstand with a roof above it like the dome in Granny Regurgita's tower-bedroom, and around the edge of the dance floor were lines of entertainment stalls and amusements. I could see a pink-and-yellow-striped helter-skelter slide, a carousel with multi-coloured seahorses around it, and a ferris wheel with carriages made from giant clams.

There were food wagons, and fortune-teller tents, and rows of wobbly mirrors, and all of it – absolutely everything – was covered in a thick blanket of cobwebs and dust.

'Well?' Abe said, after we'd been gazing at it all

for what seemed like an eternity. 'It might be in need of a good old clean-up, but you're all most welcome. Lovely, isn't it?'

'Och, it's a beauty!' Nancy sighed, fanning herself with her four hands.

'Yes!' Abe laughed. 'And how we partied here!'

I glanced upwards when a large cloud-like blob caught my attention as it moved around the outside of the glass walls, distracting me from my family's nattering.

'Gosh!' Mum cried. She'd spotted it too.

Everyone stared as the shape twisted and shimmered, darting this way and that, gliding up towards the top of the ceiling. For a moment, it looked like the giant blustery blizzard that had visited our hotel just a few weeks ago was out there in the depths, until, sparkling with the coloured lights from the pleasure gardens below, the entire cloud dived straight through the glass walls and I saw it was an immense shoal of fish!

'How did they do that?' Dad gasped. 'Are they ghosts?'

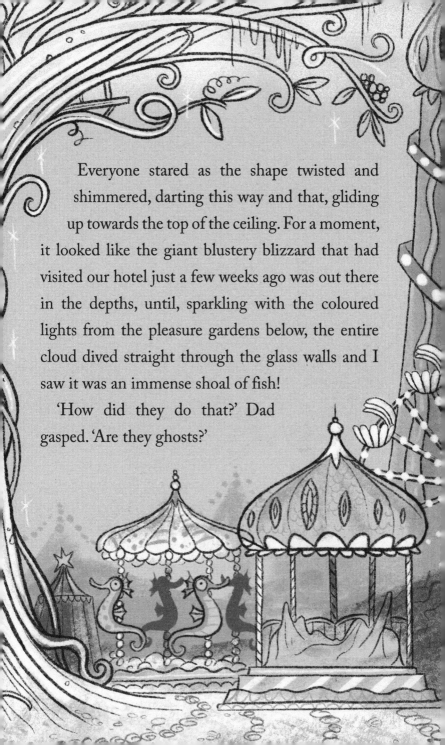

'Ha ha! What nonsense,' Abe scoffed. 'No, Bargeous, they're not spook-salmon.'

'But they just swam through solid walls!' Mum joined in. 'And now … well…' Mum pointed with a look of amazement on her face. The hundreds of little fish were soaring through the air like birds.

'Ah! That's where you've got it wrong, my friends,' Abe replied. 'I know what you're thinking, but this place isn't made from glass.'

'It's not?' Maudlin grunted. The novelty of discovering the ballroom was wearing thin and I could see she was getting grumpy again. 'Well, you could have fooled this old flubberchub! What are you talking about, you phantom fool?'

'We're standing inside a bubble. It's enchanted with mer-magic, so the local sea life can swim straight through it as though they're still in water. Marvellous, if you ask me.'

Abe floated to the nearest end of the railway

platform, then turned and beckoned for me to follow him.

'See, Frankie?' he said. 'Give it a go.'

I ran over to where my great-great-great-grandad was waiting and gently touched the see-through walls. They were cool and slightly squidgy.

'Now, one gentle push,' Abe instructed.

I couldn't help whooping with excitement as my hand passed straight through, into the warm waters on the outside. I wriggled my fingers and watched as tiny bubbles formed along them, tingling and popping.

**'THAT'S AMAZING!'** I shouted and shoved my whole arm through the wall. I could feel a gentle pull from the deep currents that were swirling around out there in the dark. It tugged at my wrist and rippled my shirt cuff.

'Not too far, my boy,' Abe said. 'You don't want to slip and end up on the wrong side.'

I pulled my arm back in,
then turned to Mum and Dad and waved
to show them my soaking wet sleeve.

'BRILLIANT!'

We watched as more and more sea
creatures glided through the walls
and emerged from
their hiding

places, attracted
by our unexpected
appearance in the bubble.

There were brightly-coloured schools
of clown fish that darted around the abandoned
food wagons, and stingrays that swooped in and
skimmed the shiny floor like fast-moving pancakes.
Herds of spiny sea dragons ventured out from
among the branches of the silver tree, rabbitfish
chased each other around the carousel, and a green
sea turtle flapped lazily over our heads.

'Get away!' a cracked voice suddenly yelped

behind me, ruining the magic of the moment. I turned to see Maudlin Maloney swatting at a large eel-like creature that was trying to nibble at the bundle of trinkets tied to her belt. 'Be off with yer!'

'Oh! I wouldn't do that if I were you,' Grandad Abe said, raising his hands as the ancient leprechaun started batting at the ugly thing. 'That's a lesser-spotted-blurtle! They go pop if they're attac—'

*BOOM! SPLAT! SQUELCH, SLOP!*

Maloney planted a hefty **WALLOP** right between the blurtle's eyes and the unfortunate creature exploded in a cloud of

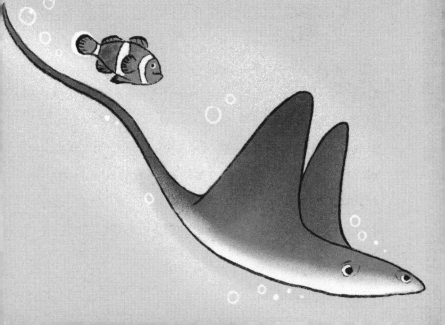

slime, showering the grizzly bad-luck fairy in strings of ooze and blobs of stinky … I don't know what.

Anyway … it doesn't take a genius to guess that Maudlin was absolutely hopping mad about it. I wanted to laugh so much, but I wouldn't have dared in a bajillion years.

'Are you okay?' Mum asked nervously as the leprechaun flicked a chunk of blurtle from the end of her stumpy nose.

Maloney didn't speak. She just stood there, dripping in sea gunk.

'Looks like it's sushi for dinner,' Nancy whispered to me, stifling a giggle.

Maudlin balled her hands into fists and scowled at the rest of us.

'I think I'm done with all the nicey-niceness, Abraham,' she croaked. 'Forget the blunkin' fish! Forget the **BLUNKIN'** fun!

'Now, now, Maudlin,' Abe said. 'Plenty more to see.'

With that, Grandad Abe hurried off down the stairs, and we all followed before the furious leprechaun could argue.

Nobody wanted to stick around beside her just then. There were wisps of smoke coming out of her ears.

## SOMETHING A LITTLE BIT STRANGE

Great-Great-Great-Grandad Abraham led us down the steps from the station platform and floated out across the room.

'I'll show you the best bits,' he said, doing his best I'm-not-worried smile at Maudlin Maloney.

We all followed, quietly gawping as we took the place in. It was even more impressive now that we were down below the towering bubble dome.

As we got closer to the silver tree in the middle of the dance-floor, I saw there were tiny, intricate houses hanging among its branches. They looked like miniature palaces with turrets and verandas and staircases looping around their outside walls ... and just when we were walking beneath the nearest

one, I spotted a tiny figure hurrying out onto a low balcony.

'Excuse me!' it squeaked. 'You there!'

Everyone stopped in their tracks and looked up. It was a miniscule piskie princess, dressed in fancy caterpillar-silk robes with a teensy crown made from bent paperclips on her head.

'I say ... who is in charge here?' she chirped.

We all turned to Abe and pointed.

'Ummm ... well, I suppose I am,' he mumbled.

'Ah, good. Allow me to introduce myself.' The piskie maiden drew herself up and tried to look as important and stern as someone the size of a thumb can do. 'I am Viscera Von Tangle of the Lower Lumplands. Princess of the Piskish, Soverign of the Squatlings...'

I caught sight of Maudlin Maloney pulling a

face. Magical royalty, no matter what species, always like to make such a song and dance about introductions.

'Empress of the Umpers, Duchess of the Dongles. And I'd like to lodge a complaint.'

'A complaint?' Abe said.

'Yes!' the princess snapped. 'I ordered room service ninety-four years ago and it still hasn't arrived!'

Grandad Abe opened his mouth to speak but the tiny figure raised an even tinier hand and stopped him.

'I'm a very patient piskie, but salamander skin paté on baked conker crackers does **NOT** take that long to prepare, no matter how good it is!'

'Ah, I see,' Abe said. 'I'll make sure that's sorted for you.' He nodded at Nancy, who pulled a small pad from her flowery apron pocket and made a note.

'Make sure you do, Mr … who are you?' the princess barked.

'Abraham Banister.'

'Lies! You are not!'

'Yes, I am!' Abe shouted back at the little thing, slightly too angrily.

'Don't try to fool me, wretched rotling! You can't prankify a piskie, don't you know? I spent many a summer with good old Abe and you are **NOT** him! I smell the green-eyed monster! You've brought it back! **YOU ARE—**'

'**A GHOST!**' Grandad Abraham blurted, stopping the princess mid-sentence. 'I know! **SURPRISE!** Nothing to worry about! Lots has changed! **MUST HURRY!**'

With that, he turned and floated off in the direction of the helter-skelter slide as fast as he could.

'Piskies!' he finally chuckled to us over his shoulder as we all rushed to catch up with the old spook. 'Such little heads! Their brains can't cope with too many thoughts at once. What a muddle-pot!'

。O。

Now, I know what you're thinking. You're saying to

yourself: **'THAT WAS WEIRD!'** and you're right
… it was! That moment with Viscera Von Tangle
brought back my little tingle of worry and started
me wondering if Abe wasn't being entirely truthful
about something. And it didn't take long to find
out what.

## ABRAHAM'S OFFICE

By the time we reached the other side of the Briny Ballroom, I could tell Mum and Dad thought something seemed a bit odd too, and they were whispering to each other. I think Dad was just getting ready to question Grandad Abe about what the piskie princess had said, when the old ghost interrupted us all.

'We're here!' he cooed merrily.

Abe was floating above a shiny circular symbol on the floor, right between the helter-skelter slide and the seahorse carousel. It was about the same size as the rug in my bedroom that Hoggit loves to roll on and scratch his scales, and as we got closer, I could see it was the shiny emblem of a wreath of twisty octopus tentacles, a bit like the ones that had appeared on the reception desk earlier that morning.

'This way,' Abe said, ushering me to stand on the gleaming shape. 'There's something I want you to see. One at a time!'

I stepped onto it and waited for something to happen, but nothing did…

'What's occurrinating?' Maudlin griped.

'I want to show you my office,' Abraham said. 'It's marvellous!'

Maudlin glanced about grumpily. I could tell she'd lost her patience for all this exploring.

'This isn't an office!' she blurted.

'No…' Abe replied, then gestured to something above and behind us. 'But that is!'

'Well, I never!' Mum beamed, following his ghost finger. 'Whatever next?'

Abe was pointing to a large platform nestled in the highest branches of the tree in the middle of the dance-floor. It had been completely hidden from view when we were over near the Atilantus station, but from here I could clearly see shelves packed with dusty books, desks and globes, framed maps, charts and bizarre clockwork gadgets hanging on chains, all nestled among the silver sculpted leaves, like the most unusual treehouse I'd ever laid my peepers on.

'What's up there?' I asked.

'Lots of things,' said Abe. 'If there's one place you might find out more about… about…'

'Oculus?' Dad asked.

'Yes,' Grandad Abe said, as a look of sadness crept across his face. 'If there are any clues about Oculus, they'll be there in my office.'

A pang of curiosity sparked inside my chest and I smiled reassuringly at the old ghost.

'Righty ho,' Abe said. 'You just need to stand on the symbol, face the Under-Oak and say in a nice clear voice, **"UPSIDE OUT, INSIDE DOWN!"'**

'What a load of **NONKUMBUMPS!**' Maloney scoffed. 'I've never heard such grumblish.'

'I'm afraid it's the only way to get up there,' Grandad Abe said.

Before Maudlin could moan for another second,

I planted my feet wide, glanced up at Abe's tree-office and shouted the special words.

'UPSIDE OUT, INSIDE DOWN!'

Almost instantly, the tentacles on the symbol beneath my feet started twitching and moving. Then, before I could wriggle free, they snaked up around my ankles and waist and lifted me high into the air.

'FRANKIE!' Mum yelped in fright as they stretched and wriggled, longer and longer.

'It's quite safe,' Abe chuckled. 'Nothing to panic over, Rani.'

I gave Mum a reassuring grin as the glinting octopus arms carried me right out over the ballroom and put me gently down on the mosaic floor of Abe's office, high up on the boughs of the metal oak.

Then, in no time at all, the slithery feelers, covered in shining sucker-pads, started shrinking back towards the floor and quickly returned to nothing but the flat symbol where I'd just been standing.

'Who's next?' Abe asked.

Fast-forward to a few minutes later and we had all been hauled, one at a time, to the balcony in the branches.

The only living person who didn't need to use the strange octopus-lift was Nancy. After the almighty fuss that Maudlin had made as she was dangling in the air, screaming: **'DON'T LOOK AT MY BUMLY-BITS! I'M WARNING YOU!!'** our spider-cook decided to fling a rope of web over the nearest branch and climb up into the tree herself.

'And here we are,' Abe said, floating up to join us once Dad had made it safely into the tree, last of all. The spook smiled nervously and peered around his cobwebby old office like there were things up here he was worried about seeing again. 'Who's for a stroll down memory lane?'

## TREASURES IN THE COBWEBS

We each scuttled off in different directions, eager to have a scrabble around Grandad Abe's office.

As much as I wanted to find out more about my Great-Great-Uncle Oculus, I was pretty excited just to be nosing about so much cool old stuff. The tree hideaway was like some sort of **MUSEUM OF THE WEIRD!** It was **TERRIFIC!!**

'What's that?' I called to Abe, pointing to a small music-box-thingy attached to a dented tin ear-trumpet. There was so much to look at, and I wanted to know about **ALL OF IT.**

'A prattle-peacer!' Abe said. 'It removes all the sound from a room with one twist of the handle. That thing proved very useful when a pod of sirens moved in and kept hypnotising us every time we tried to get them to bog-off. Turned their brain-bungling songs into perfect silence.'

'And that?' I asked, pointing to what looked like some sort of long, thin cannon that was aimed at the nearest bubble wall.

'Ah ha! That, my boy, is a perfumerator. Brilliant contraption!'

Grandad Abe floated to a cupboard next to the peculiar machine. He wriggled his fingers and the doors of it swung open.

'See in here,' he said, waving for me to join him.

Inside the little cupboard were row upon row of miniscule glass jars and each one was marked with a different sea creature's name.

'These little things contain the most powerful fish-fragrances,' Abe smiled. 'Each one will attract a different species of sea life from hundreds of miles away in a jiffy.'

I wrinkled up my forehead, not sure if he was playing a joke on me.

'It's true!' Abe chortled. 'These tiny jars are practically scent-bombs for our finny friends. You just choose which sea creature you want to look at, load the correct fragrance into the perfumerator and fire it through the bubble walls into the outside ocean. One whiff later and your favourite fish are teeming through the ballroom. It's marvellous!'

I looked down at the bottom of the cupboard and saw a whole shelf that was secured behind a tiny cage with a lock. The bottles and jars behind it were made from red glass and were glowing ominously.

'What about those ones?' I asked, pointing.

'Oooh, no!' Abe huffed. 'Not those. We never use those. They contain the stink of some of the most dangerous sea monsters on the planet. Why do you think they're all behind bars?'

I couldn't stop my eyebrows from twitching excitedly. I love reading about scary creatures from around the world ... especially ones that live under the ocean. There was a whole pile of books about them back in my bedroom.

'Don't even think about it, Frankie Banister,' Abe said, pulling his best **I'M SERIOUS!** face. 'Now be off with you. Go and see what else you can find.'

I groaned to myself and shuffled away. Never mind. I'd make sure Abe showed the perfumerator in action, at some point. I'd always wanted to see a sunfish!

Around me, tucked into the silvery branches of the giant tree, were great big cabinets with glass fronts, and they were stuffed full of the most unbelievable knick-knacks and trinkets that Abe must have picked up on his travels.

I wandered along the nearest shelf and read the faded labels on the front of the displays.

A mummified hinkapoot chieftain from Indonesia.

The toenail-clippings of an Australian bunyip.

A chess set made out of petrified plunkles from spain.

A pair of rusted metal shoes belonging to a Japanese dogu.

The carved fang of a bridge-bungle from Wales.

A wart-witch's hexing wand from Venice.

An Alaskan huskimp's spear.

A tea towel from Blackpool.

The clay mask of a wandering gnomad.

I stopped at that last artefact and juddered to myself. The mask was almost identical to the one my noggin-bonked uncle had disguised himself behind when he'd attempted to destroy the hotel.

'Och, it makes me feel squeemzy!' Nancy giggled nervously as she ogled a huge glass container of pickled pamplemoogs from France. **'BONE-JANGLING!'**

'Makes me feel right at home,' Maudlin cackled. She picked up a rattle made from a bog-bonker's crumbly old skull and waved it at Nancy. **'WOOO!** I think I knew this fella back in Dublin! **HAHA!'**

'This is incredible!' Mum exclaimed from the other side of the office. She was standing in front of a large frame, hanging between two branches of the tree. 'Frankie, guess what this is!'

I wandered over and saw it was a ginormous map of a sprawling town, filled with twisted streets and narrow alleyways. After a few seconds I shook my head and Mum pointed to four words written along the bottom of it.

'The City Of Gradibash!' she marvelled. 'That's the home of the Barrow Goblins! It's where Grogbah's from!'

Ha! I couldn't believe it! Just then I spotted, right in the centre of the map, a huge building marked: *ROYAL PALACE OF QUEEN LATRINA*.

'That's where Grog-bog grew up!' I hollered with surprise. 'I wish he'd go back!'

'Never mind that little whelpling,' Dad chuckled from the middle of the room. 'Look at this!'

I glanced in his direction, then instantly burst out laughing. Dad had been rummaging through a trunk of moth-eaten clothes and had dressed himself up in a tatty old cloak with strange trollish

The City of GRADIBASH!

runes all over it.

'I wonder what this does?' He laughed. 'How do I look?'

'Gonktious!' Mum snickered back, blowing him a kiss.

'I feel like a wizard! Ooh, there's more!' Dad dropped the cloak back into the wooden chest and snatched up a woolly yellow hat with blue trim and a red pom-pom on top. 'What's this one?'

'That doesn't look very exciting!' Mum said.

'I don't know,' Dad replied, pulling the knitted hat onto his head. 'I quite like … *AAAAAAAAGGGHHH!!!*'

The second the little cap was on his noggin, my dad shot straight into the air like a human firework. He rocketed upwards out of the tree and didn't stop until he bashed his head on one of the golden claws that held the Briny Ballroom's bubble walls in place, then he tumbled back down to the office floor with a painful-sounding *HUMPH!*

'Oh, good gracicles!' Nancy screamed. 'Bargeous, are y'all right?'

Dad stumbled to his feet and yanked the woolly hat off.

'Ugh!' he groaned, leaning giddily on the wooden trunk. 'I'm fine … I … I think … wha … what was that?'

Everyone turned to Grandad Abe for answers, but the old spook now had his back to us, staring at something in a gloomy cobwebbed corner.

'Abraham?' Nancy called, but he didn't seem to hear.

'OI!' Maudlin bellowed even louder. 'Are you snizzling or something?'

Abe slowly turned his head and saw Dad looking dazed and winded with the yellow bobble-hat in his hand.

'Oh,' the ghost mumbled. 'You should be careful with that, it's a Siberian gripe-hoof's flying cap.'

'Well, I know that now!' Dad wheezed. 'You could have warned me, Abe … Abe?'

Dad frowned. Great-Great-Great-Grandad Abe had already turned away again and was glaring back to the corner of the room. Whatever was over there had made the elderly spook completely miss all this chaos.

'Is everything okay?' Mum asked.

'What is it, Mr Banister?' Maudlin joined in.

Grandad Abe stayed silent for what seemed like a very long time, and then...

'I need to show you something,' he said.

## THE GRAVEGHAST'S CURSE

We all crowded around Abe to get a good look at what he was staring at.

'Gosh!' was all the old ghost mumbled.

He was standing in front of a tall alcove which was filled with picture frames hammered to the branches of the tree. The narrow space was absolutely stuffed-full of them. There must have been more than fifty, and they each contained old, yellowing photographs of...

'Oculus and Olympia,' Abe whimpered.

There, behind the glass of every frame, Oculus Nocturne stared out at us like a phantom and next to him stood his tall, thin mother. The hairs on the back of my neck stood on end and I could almost hear my great-great-uncle's high-pitched laughter ringing across my memory.

'You *do* remember them, don't you?' Nancy asked Abe.

'I … ummmm …' Abe's shoulders sagged miserably. 'Yes, I do.'

'Wait a foozle-farting minute!' Maudlin barked. 'Are you telling us that all your "I've forgotten" malarkey was a bunch of liarly tra-la-la-ing?'

'Not entirely,' Grandad Abe said. He turned to face us, then held up his hands as if he was expecting us to attack. 'There are bits I forgot, but not everything. It's just … it's just …'

'It's just what?!' said Mum sternly. 'What are you hiding?'

'It's just … **I COULDN'T SAY ANYTHING IN FRONT OF REGURGITA! SHE GETS SOOOOO JEALOUS!'**

Nobody spoke for a moment.

'Eh?' Dad blurted, after shaking his head in disbelief. 'I don't understand.'

'Returning to the hotel last night was

overwhelping! I hadn't seen my schmoopsy-poo in years and years! So, when you all started asking me questions I naturally wanted to tell you everything right away, but I just couldn't. It would upset my honey-blossom **SO MUCH,** and she was already very cross! I hoped … no … I knew if I just showed you my office, I could prove to you all I wasn't a

cowardly cankle without talking about it in front of Regurgita.'

'**YOU FIBBLER!**' Maloney yelled.

'I know,' Abe sighed. 'But I so wanted you all to trust me. It's not every day a ghost meets his great-great-great relatives.'

'So, you remember everything about that horrible night?' Mum asked. 'You poor thing.'

'Of course I can recall my beloved Olympia and little Oculus.' Grandad Abe said. 'But I don't really recall very much about when the graveghast bewitched them. Being a ghost means your memories are hazy at best and I confess I've been a tad worried about what we might find here.'

We all watched as Abe picked up a picture frame and stared at it. His face was a complete muddle of emotions.

'To my relief, this picture proves I didn't run away like Oculus told you. He got that bit wrong.'

'I always believed you,' Dad said.

'It's all coming back to me now … hexes like that affect different people in different ways. My dear sweet Olympia was turned into a toad! They were her least favourite animal in the whole world, including flatulence-wumps, and it must have unbearable for her. I … got off rather more lightly. When that foul fairy cast her spell, it seems I was setting up my old camera a little way off and was protected from the worst of it.'

'So, what happened to you?' I asked.

'My memory was wiped clean as a whistle, and when I woke up in the reeds, I couldn't remember anything after the moment we arrived at that grizzly old graveghast's lair near the river. Not a jot!'

'That's awful!' Mum gasped.

'Believe me, I know!' Abe replied. 'My wife and child were gone, but I know what happened to them now because … well, you can see for yourself.'

The old ghost turned the floating photo frame around in mid-air and Mum took hold of it gently.

'Oh, Abraham,' she sobbed, then passed the photo to Maloney who handed it round in turn.

Inside the picture frame was a stained, cracked photograph showing … ugh! This is seriously brain-bungling, so brace yourself, my reader friend! It was a photo of the exact moment the graveghast unleashed her horrible curse. **BLEUUGH!!**

The death fairy was right in the middle of the picture, with Oculus in the background, screaming and turning to run. Lightning crackled between him and the graveghast's outstretched hand as she blew a kiss, and Olympia Nocturne was halfway between transforming from a prim-looking lady into a bloated-bumpish-froggy-thing. I don't think you need to hear anything else about that really … except that Abe was clearly visible, lying unconscious among the reeds in the bottom corner. He hadn't run away like a wimpus. He'd been telling the truth.

'I must have clicked the shutter as I was knocked out,' Abe said, looking sadder and more confused by the second. 'If I remember correctly, I searched and searched and searched for months, but I found nothing. Eventually I had to return to England, convinced that Oculus and Olympia were long-gone.'

'And then what happened?' I asked.

'I met the carbuncled-beauty, Regurgita Glump.'

I grimaced at the thought of someone thinking Granny was beautiful, and Mum nudged me as she spotted it.

'I never thought I'd be happy again after that sad tragedy, so you can imagine how jumbly it felt when I got to marry a magical, and we built this wonderful hotel together.'

'So, all this time, you thought your wee boy had popped his clonkers,' Nancy blubbed, dabbing tears

from the corners of her eight eyes.'

'My memories are moth-eaten, but I'm certain I **NEVER** stopped trying to find him in secret,' Abe added. 'I recall sending out thousands of letters via Goblin Post, but Regurgita would get so green and jealous, her moods would terrify away all the guests.'

'That's what the piskie princess must have meant when she said you'd brought back the green-eyed monster,' I said. 'I've figured it out!'

'Yes! That's it, my boy, and she'd be right if I'd mentioned Oculus up there in the hotel foyer!' Abe agreed. 'Regurgita once punched a puddle-nymph right through the front door for kindly asking if I'd heard anything about my son! She only let me keep the portrait of me and Oculus hanging in reception because she was too lazy to climb up and tear it down. That's why all my other findings and photographs are down here, I suppose, where my schmoopsy-poo never comes. It doesn't stop me loving her, though! She's so adorable!'

'Hang on!' Mum suddenly blurted. 'That's all sorted, then!'

'What, Rani?' Nancy asked.

'He's completely innocent! Abraham was never a cruminal or a grobskwonking old gonk. Everything's **FINE!**'

'You're right!' Dad cheered. 'Abraham! It's done!'

'That's that, then!' Mum yelped, jumping up and down on the spot. 'We need to think big for tonight's party. **REALLY BIG!**'

'Promise me one thing,' Abe suddenly blurted.

'Promise me we can have the party down here in the ballroom.'

'Oh,' Dad mumbled. 'Abe, I don't think we could get it ready in time for tonight. It's filthy and everything's covered in dust.'

**'PLEASE!'** Grandad Abe pleaded. 'It would mean the worlds to me! I want to see everyone partying down here, the whole hotel and all the family. **PLEASE!**'

A look of determination spread across Mum's face.

'What are enchanted mops and an eager team of home-sweet-home-hobs for?' she laughed.

'Let's do it!'

'Oh, Rani! That's the spirit! My spookerish heart is filled with so much love for you all!' Abe cheered.

'Steady on now, Mr Banister,' Maudlin grimaced, backing away as fast as possible. 'We're not going to hug are we?'

## PHEWY!!

Congratulations, my human friend! You've made it to chapter nineteen of my story!

I bet you didn't think you'd have stuck with me for this long after reading about grouchy grannies and moaning magicals, but I promised things would get a lot more exciting, and I knew you could tell I wasn't fibbing, even if Great-Great-Great-Grandad Abraham was ... ha!

But it's not over yet! There's plenty more to come. Just you wait...

## TIME TO CELEBRATE!

I'd never seen Mum and Dad look so excited in my life!

Without another word, we all rushed to the Atilantus station, and were all speeding back towards dry land before you could shout, '**IT'S GOING TO BE THE GRANDEST PARTY EVER!**'

By the time we made it to the circular lift below reception and had trundled our way up above ground, all the plans were in place. One or two of our super nosy guests were still straggling about and they jumped to attention as they spotted us rising through the floor.

'**WE'RE GOING TO HAVE THE BIGGEST**

SHINDIG THE HOTEL HAS EVER SEEN!'
Mum shouted, frantically pacing about and flapping like a crazed rooster. 'EVERYTHING OCULUS SAID WAS A LIE!'

'Let's invite everyone we can think of and all the non-human newspapers!' Dad whooped. 'The whole magical world will want to know that Abraham is back and we have a ballroom! AN UNDERSEA BALLROOM! AGAIN! We'll be the envy of enchanted hotels everywhere.'

In no time, Mum was standing on the stone reception desk, barking orders.

'Nancy, you're in charge of food! Make it a feast they'll never forget!'

'Aye-aye, Rani!' Nancy giggled and sprinted off towards the kitchen. 'I've got a recipe for manatee mucus meringue I've been dying to try!!'

'Maudlin, you're on party bags! Can you fill a few hundred with lucky charms and the odd hex for a bit of a surprise?'

'I'll see what I can rustle up!' Maloney cackled and waddled off to her lepre-caravan in the corner of the foyer. 'I'm sure I can find some real shockers!'

'Abraham!'

'Yes?' The ghost was definitely startled to hear his name called.

'You … ummm … you can just relax! You'll be our guest of honour this evening! So why don't you pop off to the mud spa or something? I'm sure even ghosts can enjoy a dip!' Mum shouted like an over-eager sergeant major.

'Oh, lovely!' Abe said.

'Bargeous!' Mum squawked, as Dad jolted and started to look a bit nervous. 'Gather the enchanted mops and all the home-sweet-home hobs and get them back down to the ballroom, **PRONTO!!** We want that place gleaming like it was built yesterday!'

'Okay, darling!' Dad said, spinning on his heels and running for the cleaning cupboard.

'I'll sort out invitations and muster the staff,' Mum blurted, thinking aloud. 'Frankie? **FRANKIE?!'**

○ ⭕ ○

What!?!? You don't think I stuck around to be

given a list of chores, do you?

No way! I'm not nogginbonked!

By the time Mum was ordering Dad to go sort out the cleaning, I was already sneaking off to my secret bedroom above the library to tell my best, best, **BESTEST** pet pygmy soot-dragon all about what had happened that day.

**PERFECT!!**

## HIDING FROM CHORES

As my armchair lift rattled up through the floor of my room, I felt practically giddy with happiness.

Knowing for certain that Abe was innocent and I'd just been a big Worrying-Wilfred was wonderful. Great-Great-Great-Grandad Abraham really was just as much of the brilliant hero I'd always thought him to be.

Suddenly everything in my dusty bedroom seemed new. The portrait of Abe and Oculus above the fireplace didn't make me squirm with worry and confusion. All the piles of books felt more exciting... like I was one step closer to actually seeing some of the amazing things inside them for real, and I had that warm glow in my tummy, knowing that tonight we were going to have a proper Bulch/Banister celebration to welcome the newest (and oldest, I guess) member of the family.

Oh! Speaking of warm glows...

'Hoggit!' I whispered to the fireplace. 'Come on, boy, wake up. We're going to have a party!'

The coals in the bottom of the grate shifted and my favourite creature in the whole hotel opened one eye, then stretched a stumpy leg lazily into the air.

'You won't believe the things that have happened today!'

Scooping the little dragon out of the fireplace, I carried him to the bed, and opened one of the big books I'd been looking at the night before. It was an anthology of rare animals.

'What do you want to read about today?' I asked, glancing down the page. 'Nightgorms? Grimagonks? Spectrils?'

Hoggit puffed out a little line of smoke rings.

'Spectrils, eh?' I said, scratching the little dragon under the chin. 'A spectril is the ghost of someone or something still living that has escaped its body. A shapeshifter, it can be forced back to its host if touched by a genuine ghost. Spooky!'

I flicked through a few more pages until I found a chapter on magical sea life.

'Oooh! I saw one of those today,' I laughed, pointing to an illustration of a lesser-spotted-blurtle. 'It exploded all over Maudlin Maloney when she whacked it right on the nose!'

Hoggit rolled onto his back on my duvet and puffed out another row of tiny smoke rings. He loves it when I read to him.

Turning the page, I gasped.

The next chapter was all about monsters of the deep. I thought about Abe's perfumerator machine and the tiny bottles of red glass as I read about some of the great big nasties that were lurking out there in the oceans...

For the next few hours, that's all me and Hoggit did. Even Grogbah left us alone. He spent the entire afternoon skinny-dipping in the foyer fountains instead of trying to irritate me. **BLISS!!**

## Whip-Slicer Eel:

Covered in razor-like scales, the whip-slicer eel is known to grow up to twenty metres in length and can cut straight through the hull of a fishing boat like it was butter.

**Location: South China Sea**

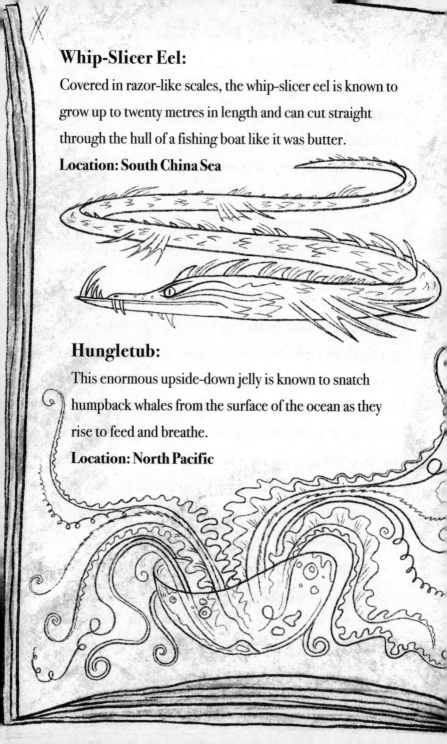

## Hungletub:

This enormous upside-down jelly is known to snatch humpback whales from the surface of the ocean as they rise to feed and breathe.

**Location: North Pacific**

## Medusa Shrimp:

Colossal in size, this bottom-dweller has been known to cause earthquakes with its constant burrowing and digging for food along the ocean floor.

**Location: Bay of Bengal, Indian Ocean**

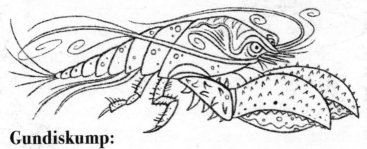

## Gundiskump:

A gargantuan fish, known for eating anything it comes across. Lures prey with a glowing light growing on a stalk from its forehead. Mature adults have been known to swallow whole villages right from the seashore.

**Location: Atlantic Ocean, Baltic Sea and North Sea.**

But it wasn't long after nightfall that the Yell-O-Phone started crackling away and I could hear Mum barking more instructions from the kitchen. It sounded like the whole hotel was in party-planning panic!

From the sounds of things, Dad had only just made it back from his second long trip to the Briny Ballroom with the home-sweet-home hobs and he was now hurriedly sending out all of Mum's invitations via a constant queue of goblin messengers from the sky door, and prawny-postmen from the sea door.

Ooof had been ordered to carry all the crates of frog-grog down to the Atilantus, ready for our guests later that evening.

Though there was one member of the family who was not happy about the party **AT ALL!** Granny Regurgita was **FURIOUS** that we'd opened up the other half of the hotel! I overheard Mum trying to explain to her that Abe was definitely not a lily-livered lumpling and we were going to throw him a party, but Granny just screamed, *'OH,*

*BOG OFF, YOU BUNCH OF NINKUMPOOPERS! I HOPE THE SNACKS GO OFF AND YOU ALL GET SQUITTLY!'*

Now can you see why I sneaked off when I did? Ha ha!

## THE GRAND RE-OPENING

By the time eight o'clock arrived, I'd finally got changed into my smartest bell-hop outfit, and I could already hear the rumble of distant chatter from our excited hotel guests in the foyer. The celebration was about to begin.

I hurried back down to the ground floor on the armchair lift, then ran out of the library to the grand reception hall, and…

**EVERYWHERE I LOOKED, THERE WAS PANDEMONIUM!**

The foyer was absolutely crammed with guests, dressed in their best party outfits and enthusiastically nattering as they lined up to be on the next lift-load down to the Atilantus station.

'Cooee! Frankie!' the Molar Sisters called when they spotted me in the doorway. 'Thith ith tho exthiting!'

'Whoever heard of an undersea shindig?' Gadys Potts howled. 'It's the best thing ever. I can't wait for a doggy-paddle!'

'Have you seen my mum or my dad?' I shouted to the geriatric tooth fairies and their werepoodle chum. They all pointed towards the reception counter, scratching ears and grinning gappy grins.

Sure enough there was Dad, standing on the stone block and looking extremely flustered. He was clutching Mum's special door key in his hand and was trying his best to manage the lift.

'Don't push!' he snapped at an impatient boggart who'd just elbowed a family of moss gremlins aside, sending the stumpy things sprawling across the tiles. 'Yes! There's room for everyone. No one will be left behind, don't worry. Mrs Blink, there's really no reason for hysterics ... no, you can't bring your bed with you!'

Dad spotted me and waved.

'Frankie, you'd better hop on and get to the ballroom,' he called. 'Your mum is already down there with Ooof and Nancy. Who knows what chaos they're dealing with?'

'Excuse me,' I said to an angry-looking hobyah as she shuffled and struggled her way to the front of the line. She tutted loudly as I stepped onto the circular lift before her.

'GOING DOWN!' Dad yelled. 'NEXT STOP, THE ATILANTUS!'

With that, he turned the key on the octopus lock and the lift-full of mumbling magicals began to lower into the floor.

When we arrived down at the station platform, it was just as busy as the hotel reception.

'Good luck!' Dad said to me with a wink, before returning up to the ground floor above.

Everywhere I looked there were crowds of eager guests, shoving and jostling to get their seat on the constant stream of fish-skeleton carriages that rattled back and forth along the tracks.

I was about to duck around the elderly pine

dryad, who was fussing with a pink bowtie he was trying to fasten around his trunk-neck, when I spotted Abe floating at the end of the wooden walkway.

'Grandad Abe!' I hollered above the loud babble of our gossiping guests, but he didn't seem to hear me. I darted through the throng of people and ran up to my ghost grandad. 'Abe, we should get down to the Briny Ballroom. You don't want to be late for your own welcoming party.'

But Abe didn't move. He was staring at himself in a battered mirror that hung on the side of the dilapidated ticket kiosk. It was one of those wiggly ones that made you look warped and lumpy.

'I never imagined I'd see this place again,' he sighed without looking away from his reflection. Instead, the old ghost smiled at me in the mirror. We both appeared weirdly swirly with giant middles, like we'd both grown super big bellies. 'It's a funny thing, coming back to haunt a place, but finding there are lots of memories haunting you right back.'

I nodded, then opened up my mouth to speak, but stopped myself when I spotted that in his reflection, Abe's left eye was green.

'Ah, you noticed it too.' Abe said, seeing me frown.

'Puzzling, no? Looking glasses are strange things. They often show us truths we can't see on our own.'

'But … why?' I stammered. 'Why do you have one eye like Oculus?'

'Who can say?' Abe said, turning around to face me. I glanced up at him and saw both his eyes were blue away from the mirror.

'I suppose it's a little bit of history showing through the cracks, reminding me not to forget my son.' Abe looked sad for a moment.

'Come on, Grandad!' I grinned my biggest grin and did my best to shake the glum ghost out of his mood. 'There's a party in the Briny Ballroom in your honour! You're getting the welcome you always wanted.'

Abe's face creased into a smile.

'You're right!' he laughed. 'What am I doing

here moping at a mirror? Let's go, Frankie. A night to remember awaits!'

## THE BOTTOM OF THE SEA BALL

'Would you look at that!' Great-Great-Great-Grandad Abraham chuckled as we stepped (and floated) out through the Atilantus's shining ribs onto the arrivals platform. **'TERRIFIC!'**

I glanced up and felt like I might burst into tears for the billionth time that day. The Briny Ballroom looked completely different. All the cobwebs and the dust that covered every surface was gone, leaving everything shimmering and glinting in the warm, golden glow of the giant coral-shaped candelabra that lined the stairs. The home-sweet-home hobs had worked a complete miracle!

Below us, the ballroom teemed with life. Music from the bandstand filled the air as an orchestra of anemanonks plucked at bizarre stringed instruments with their many pink and orange feelers, and the gleaming dance floor swirled with guests as they waltzed around the Under-Oak.

I could barely stop myself from staring! Magicals can sniff out a shindig from miles away and it looked as though half the ocean had turned up to celebrate.

Mergullies (jellymaidens from the darkest depths, and the builders who helped Abe construct the Atilantus) danced gracefully through the air, and kulpies splashed about in the fountains that were now exploding with jets of water.

A pod of swelkies, with their half-man, half-lobster bodies, stamped out an intricate tap dance on one of the balconies and a party of dazzling mermaids galloped through the ceiling of the bubble, riding on coral-spiked hippocamps.

'Ooh! It'th gorgeouth!' a familiar voice blurted right behind me, as Dentina Molar flopped off the newest Atilantus carriage to arrive and nearly knocked me straight over the railing of the platform.

'Come and look at thith, girlth!'

More and more of our regular guests came bundling past me, pushing and shoving down the staircases to get closer to the action. Berol Dunch was so excited to discover she could swim through the air down here, she shot straight through Grandad Abe without so much as an **EXCUSE-ME!**

'I think it's time we joined in the fun,' I said as Abe looked at me with a slightly bewildered expression.

'I think you're right, my boy. Quick, before someone else makes a dash through me. Ha!'

As we headed into the crowd, I caught sight of more and more **TERRIFIC** things. This party was even better than **TROGMANAY!**

Jars filled with twinkling plankton had been hung in the branches of the tree in the middle of the room, and everywhere I turned, I could see Nancy's most delunctious treats and tummy-tinkling nibbles being carried about on enchanted trays that bobbed and swooped through the dancing couples.

'Frankie! There you are!'

I spun around and saw Mum awkwardly waltzing with Ooof.

'Isn't this lovely?' she said, grimacing as our handyogre stepped on her toe.

'Squibbly!' I said, feeling slightly frazzled.

'Did you see the carousel?' Mum asked. 'It scrubbed up beautifully!'

I looked over and saw the carousel polished and shining with hundreds of little electric lights as it went in circles.

**'OH, I DO LIKE TO BE BENEATH THE SEASIDE!'** Nancy had finished her cooking for the evening and had somehow clambered onto one of the wooden seahorses. She was singing happily to herself, kicking her four legs back and forth as she rode the small thing around and around.

'Ooof managed to get the old generators going. Didn't you, Ooof?' said Mum. 'And the fountains!'

The ogre grinned and trod on Mum's toe again. **'HELLO, FRANKIE!'** he beamed.

'You two have fun,' Mum said. 'But don't go far. It's nearly time for your speech, Abe.'

'My speech?' Abe gasped.

'Of course, silly!' Mum laughed. 'Everyone's here to celebrate the return of you and the Briny Ballroom. You have to say a little something or they'll all be disappointed.'

Great-Great-Great-Grandad Abe nodded slowly and turned away, deep in thought.

'Great!' said Mum. Then she leaned in close to me and whispered, 'Oh, and, Frankie, if you see your father or Maudlin, let them know it's nearly speech time, will you? I want lots of familiar faces to be together, so we can support your grandfather.'

With that, she turned back to Ooof and they waltzed clumsily away, mouthing, *'ONE, TWO, THREE ... OUCH, TWO, THREE ... ONE, TWO, OUCH...'*

## WHAAAAAAATT!?!?

Grandad Abe excused himself politely and floated off to his tree house office to have a think about what he was going to say in his speech, leaving me to wander by myself.

'Young man!' a little voice squeaked just above my head as I passed beneath the Under-Oak, dodging dancing couples in all directions. 'Young man, I have something important to tell you!'

I looked up and saw it was Princess Viscera Von Tangle on her balcony. She was waving frantically, but I pretended I hadn't heard her over the music. I wasn't about to start off my evening with a bunch of complaints from a pompous piskie.

'Young man, you must listen!'

The busiest part of the amusement stands were the snack carts and game stalls and I headed straight for them, leaving the princess chirping behind me.

I love going to Brighton Pier with Nancy on the odd occasion she has a bit of free time from the kitchens and can glimmer herself for a morning. It's always noisy and bustling and jam-packed with rides and things to see, but this was so much better! I swear to you, my reader friend. Magicals seriously know how to have a good time.

'Get your lucky charms!' I heard a scratchy voice yelling as I turned the corner next to a food cart where a giant purple octopus was flipping seaweed pancakes.

I wandered past a game stall with the words, **'DUNK THE DUGONG'** written above it, and an open tent where a reef-nymph was reading the palm of a nervously twitching dolphumble, and then ... I found the owner of the voice.

'Got callouses on your crustaceans? I can fix 'em!'

It was Maudlin. Somehow, she'd got her entire lepre-caravan and all her chickens down here and was selling her wares to a frantically jostling crowd that had gathered around the front stoop.

'Suffering with ninkumplump neighbours? Why not hex the blighters? I've got curses, bad luck tinctures, and jinxes that'll turn an urchin's spikes into spaghetti!'

I ducked low and started to squeeze through the group of shoppers.

'Down on your luck? How about a bottle of this Fail-No-More Formula?'

Almost every creature standing there was waving its

arm, or flapping a flipper, or swinging a tentacle in the air. At this rate, Maloney would be rich by morning.

'Are you uglier than a bog-bonker? You could be gonktious in seconds with one blow of this beauty-toot whistle!'

I struggled through to the front of the crowd and tried to catch the ancient leprechaun's attention.

'Got a lazy husband? Prickle his bottom with this Get-Up-Ya-Ejit spell!'

I tapped Maudlin on her foot, but the grizzly old thing was on a roll and ignored me, flicking away my hand with the toe of her curly shoe.

'Got a quarrelsome wife? Turn her into a pleasantly clucking hen! That's what I did!'

Maloney's chickens all squawked and flapped their wings from the rusted-penny roof of the lepre-caravan.

'Settle down, ladies!' she croaked.

'Maudlin!' I poked her foot again. 'Maudlin!'

'**WHAT?**' the grizzly old grunion snapped.

'Mum says we all need to get together ready for

Grandad Abe's speech.'

The leprechaun rolled her eyes and wedged her stumpy fists against her hips.

'Oh, blunkers! Why do I put up with you bunch of Banistumps?' she moaned. Then she turned to the gaggle of shoppers and yelled, 'Be off wit' yer! I'll be back in a munkle-minute or three, so I will.'

Maudlin fetched a ring of keys from her apron pocket and set about locking up her little home.

'How did you get all this down here?' I asked as she turned the lock with a rusty **CLUNK!**

'Ain't nothing Manky Old Maloney can't do,' she cackled, giving me a mischievous wink. 'Just your average shrinking charm, dontchaknow? I popped the whole thing into my coin pouch and away we went. The girls didn't like it much, but hey ho!'

We set off down the alley of stalls and carts, heading for the Under-Oak.

'This is the stuff of nonsense,' Maudlin mumbled to herself as we shuffled through the bustling merfolk.

'What is?'

'This! All this!' Maloney said, waving her hands around at the party. 'There's no way Mistress Glump is going to let that old spook hang around the hotel. A welcoming party? It's all a waste of tinkery time.'

'I think it's brilliant!' I shot back at her. By now I couldn't have felt gladder that Abe was back. I'd spent all afternoon imagining the amazing things he could teach me now he was here and there was no way I was going to let Maudlin spoil it.

'You think **THIS** is brilliant?' she jeered, waving her hands at the **PIN THE TAIL ON THE SEA SLUG** stall and a whole bank of wobbly mirrors. 'You're bungled in the bonce, Frankie Banister.'

Maudlin caught sight of her reflection in the row of looking glasses and stopped in her tracks. Everyone else who was standing in front of them appeared hilarious and twisty, with giant heads or long and loopy legs, but the grizzled bad luck fairy looked pretty much the same.

I stifled a giggle, but she caught me and scowled.

'I hate mirrors!' she barked. 'Cruel things, they are! Strange and secretive and sneakerish!'

'Don't worry,' I said, patting her on her tiny shoulder. Who knew leprechauns could be sensitive?

'You're not the only one with a weird reflection. Grandad Abe had one green eye in his—'

'**WHAAAAAAATT!?**' Maudlin grabbed me by the lapel of my jacket and yanked me towards her until our noses were touching. '**WHAT DID YOU SAY?**'

'It's fine!' I grunted, pulling myself free from her gnarled hands. 'He said it was history showing through the cracks or something. That it was reminding him never to forget Oculus.'

'Abe's reflection had one green eye in the mirror? You're sure?' Maudlin hissed in my face with wild eyes.

'Yes!' I said, feeling a knot of worry and fear tie itself up in my belly.

'**FRANKIE!**' Maloney's face creased up in horror. '**GHOSTS DON'T HAVE REFLECTIONS!**'

## THE SPEECH

My brain swirled with panic as Maudlin took hold of my wrist and pulled me through the throng of partying magicals.

We darted this way that, heaving between bustling bodies until we reached the edge of the dance floor and…

*TING! TING! TING! TING!*

The noise echoed around the bubble and silenced the speedily plucking anemenonk orchestra. We all turned towards Mum and Dad, who were standing on the balcony where the swelkies had been tap dancing earlier. Mum was dinging a teaspoon against a bluebottle brandy glass and smiling sweetly down at everyone.

'Ladies and gentlemen,' Dad shouted over the room. 'We are thrilled…'

'And tooth fairies!' three lisping voices called from somewhere in the crowd.

'Yes, and tooth fairies,' Dad said.

'And werepoodles!'

'And impolumps!'

'And merfolk! Fish have feelings too!'

'EVERYONE!' Mum butted in, very familiar with how long these interruptions could go on. 'ABSOLUTELY EVERYONE!'

'We are thrilled to welcome you ALL to the grand re-opening of the Briny Ballroom and Pleasure Gardens,' Dad continued, as goblin reporters from the *Observerator* and *Daily Grimes* newspapers took photographs with old-fashioned clockwork cameras, flashing and clicking like thunderbugs.

'We have to tell them something's wrong,' I whispered to Maudlin.

She looked at me with worried eyes.

'Wait…' she said.

'As the managers of **the Nothing To See Here Hotel,**' Mum yelled, taking over from Dad, 'we couldn't be happier to be throwing a shindig in a dance hall so grand it makes us the envy of all magical hotels everywhere. And it's all thanks to one man … well … ghost!'

Mum gestured to the Under-Oak in the middle of the dance floor and everyone looked up to see

Grandad Abe floating on the veranda of his treehouse office.

'ABRAHAM BANISTER!' Dad shouted. Even from this far away, I could see he was brimming with pride.

'H-hello!' Abe said to the silent sea of upturned faces. 'It's nice to see you all. I … ummm … I don't have too much to talk about. It gives me great pride to know you're all waltzing and whirling in my honour, and I'm so happy to announce…'

I held my breath and waited for what the ghost/not-ghost was about to say. If this man wasn't a spook, what was going on? He couldn't be alive, could he?

Abe was about to finish his sentence when a tiny burst of ectoplasm exploded in the air above the fountains and… Grogbah materialised!

'AAAAAAAGH!' The little ghost reeled backwards in disgust as he instantly saw the hundreds of magicals staring at him. 'GET OUT, YOU

INTRUDLES! ALL OF
YOU!!'

'Oh, not again,
Grogbah!' Mum called
to the pumpkin-shaped
prince.

Grogbah turned in the
direction of her voice and
screamed again.

'WHAT ARE YOU DOING HERE?'

'I might ask you the same question,' Dad
shouted back.

'This is my private snoozle room, where I come
to rest and relax in peace!' Grogbah whined. 'It's
mine and you're not allowed in!'

'It's not your snoozle room!' Mum called. 'This is
the hotel ballroom. We're in the middle of a party
and you're not invited.'

'YOU CAN'T BE IN HERE!' Grogbah wailed in
his annoying little voice.

'Well, we are!' Dad replied. 'Now slunkle off …
you're spoiling Abe's speech.'

'**WHO?**' Grogbah looked like he was about to burst.

'HIM!' Dad shouted, pointing to the Under-Oak.

Grogbah spun around again.

'Oh! It's you…' he said, looking surprised when he spotted Grandad Abe. 'I thought you were all frosted up.'

'Be quiet!' Abe snapped at the goblin-ghost.

'Don't speak to me like that, you rottly skwonker!' Grogbah jabbed a chubby finger at Abe. 'You swungled me good and proper before! I demand apologiffies!'

'I'm not saying sorry to the likes of you,' Abe spat. 'You nearly spoiled everything last time and now you're ruining my speech!'

'What do you mean "last time"?' Dad yelled, silencing the argument. 'Do you two know each other?'

'**NO!**' Abe blurted.

'Of course we do!' Grogbah sneered. 'That's—'

Suddenly another explosion of ectoplasm erupted

in the air above the staircase and ... my jaw practically hit the ground.

There, floating on the other side of the dance floor was a second figure of ... of ... **GREAT-GREAT-GREAT GRANDAD ABRAHAM!**

## SEEING DOUBLE

The crowd gasped in unison as the second figure of Abe turned to face the first.

'You!' he barked. 'I might have known!'

'Don't even think about it, you slithering idiot,' the first Abe spat from the balcony in the tree. 'You're not stopping me now!'

'You can't do this!' the second Abe cried. 'It's madness!'

Watching the two identical ghosts yelling at each other was completely noggin-bonking. I started to wonder if I'd accidentally drunk some frog-grog by mistake, until I realised that everyone else could see them too.

'What's going on?' Maudlin shrieked above the

commotion. She grabbed my arm and we pushed through the crowd together. 'Explain yourself, ghost!'

The second Abe by the stairs turned to glance at us and his face lit up when he spotted Maudlin.

'Miss Maloney!' he said. 'I'm so glad you're all right. I've been very worried about you and my relatives.'

'What are you rambling on about?' the leprechaun snapped. 'Who are you?'

'I'm Abraham Banister!' the ghost blurted.

'No, he isn't!' the other Abe yelled from the tree-house. '*I'm* Abraham Banister!'

'Maudlin, you must believe me!' the second Abe pleaded from the stairs. 'I was so happy when you called last night, I truly was. What you may not realise, however, I was still on the other end of the line when I heard you all start screaming and the sound of lightning and chaos. Then I listened in horror as someone started speaking with my voice. That's when the skell-a-phone went dead and I knew you were all in grave danger.'

'Don't listen to him!' the first Abe shouted. 'He's lying!

'I'm not!' Abe number two replied. 'I hurried straight here from the Land of the Dead. The road is dark and dangerous. I've been journeying for hours!'

I watched as Maloney's face creased in concentration.

**'PROVE IT!'** she finally hollered at the identical spooks.

'Yes, of course,' the second Abe said excitedly. 'Ask me anything.'

The ancient leprechaun glanced at both the figures and scratched her chin. I could practically hear the cogs going around inside her head.

'I've known you for a long time, Abraham Banister. Well … Banisters.'

'Yes!' they both replied.

'So, I want you to tell me about your favourite time we strolled along the river in Dublin together.'

'There are so many wonderful memories,' the first Abe chuckled from the tree house. His face twitched like he was desperately wracking his brains. 'There's the time we watched the sunset, and the time you tried human ice cream. We loved feeding the swans!'

'Mmmmm,' Maudlin grunted with a nod. She turned to the second ghost and pointed at him. 'And you?'

'We never walked along the river!' he laughed. 'You hate humans, and you hate strolls, and you hate sunsets!'

**'AH HA!'** Maudlin guffawed. In a flash, she grabbed the wand from the hand of a nearby murkle-witch, pointed it at the Abraham in the Under-Oak and bellowed **'UN–DIS–COM–BUMP–U–LATE!'**

Lightning burst from the tip of the wand and split the air in two, streaking across the ballroom and exploding right in the centre of the first Abraham's chest.

It fizzed and crackled all over the old ghost, sending fingers of blue electricity snaking along the veranda railings and up into the branches of the Under-Oak.

Screams erupted from around the ballroom and magicals dropped to the ground, trying to avoid the blast.

Then…

Silence.

The blinding light vanished as quickly as it had appeared and we all glanced up to where my great-great-great-grandad had been floating only seconds before.

Sure enough, the ghost was still there in the tree, only now he was shimmering and rippling like we were looking at him through water. I watched with wide eyes as the figure started to shrink and pulsate.

**'CLEAR THE WAY!'** Maudlin screeched, and the crowds of creatures backed away in all directions, leaving me

and the leprechaun in the middle of a large circle.

'Frankie!' Mum yelped when she saw us. 'What's happening?'

'Not now, Mrs Banister,' Maudlin shouted, lifting the wand again. 'We've got bigger things to worry about.'

Everyone in the ballroom held their breath.

'Unless my papery old mind has been scrunkled, we've got ourselves a spectril!'

'A what?' I said. I knew it was a bad time for questions, but I couldn't help myself. Something about that word seemed strangely familiar.

'Regular ghosts come from humans who have popped their clonkers,' Maloney replied, squinting one eye as she aimed the wand again. 'But a spectril is the ghost of someone who's still alive.'

'Whose?' I gasped, remembering reading about spectrils in my room earlier in the day.

'Who do you think?' Maudlin huffed sarcastically. 'Look!'

I glanced up again to see black hair sprouting from the floating figure's head and an eye patch materialise over his right eye.

**'BLUNKERS!'** I heard myself yelling over the crowd's cries of alarm.

Grandad Abe's old explorer suit transformed into a black jacket with knee-high trousers, and a piercing beam of light reflected around the ballroom as the spectril's left eye flared with a green glow.

My heart rose up into my throat and I realised with terror gurgling around my belly that I was staring at my scowling, hate-filled great-great-uncle, Oculus Nocturne.

It wasn't him completely, but a yellow-grey apparition, like the photographs we'd seen earlier. The only thing of real colour on him was that piercing green eye.

'**YOU!**' Maudlin cried, as the boy floated back down to the balcony. 'I should have known!'

The real Grandad Abe's ghost stared up with a look of abject terror at the boy, and the boy slowly turned and leered back at him.

'Hello, Daddy!'

The real Abe turned to the throng of partygoers.

'A spectril can rifle through the old thoughts of the person it's changed into!' he howled. 'You're all in terrible danger!'

'Oh, shut up, you snivelling worm!' Oculus hissed at his father. 'It's too late!'

'What do you want, boy?' Maudlin yelled. 'Why have you come back here?'

Oculus glared down at me and Maloney and laughed a chilling, shrill laugh.

'Ah! My old friends!' he snickered. 'I can't tell you how much it warms my heart to see your

putrid faces.'

'Answer the question!' I yelled. **'WHY ARE YOU HERE?'**

'That's just it. I'm *not* here,' Oculus fumed. 'I'm frozen in a block of ice, stored away on top of a glacier in **THE HIMALAYAS** where you all **TRAPPED ME!'**

He clutched at the veranda railing and the entire Under-Oak suddenly bristled with great spikes of frost.

**'DO YOU HAVE ANY IDEA HOW UNBEARABLE IT IS TO BE STUCK LIKE THAT? WELL, YOU WILL WHEN I'M FINISHED WITH YOU!'**

Mum and Dad came running through the crowd and joined me and Maudlin in the clearing of creatures.

'The only good thing about being frozen solid and left to be forgotten by your own relatives,' Oculus continued, 'is you have plenty of time to think, and plan, and plot your revenge! And, oh ho ho, have I come up with a spine-jangling punishment. I was just hanging around in the ice, daydreaming about how lovely it would be to hear you all screaming, when the idea just came to me ... I might be stuck in the middle of nowhere, but I could go wherever I wanted using my

spectril. So I let it wander all the way back here, and who should I interrupt your skell-a-phone conversation with? My daddy-kins! What a **WONDERFUL** coincidence. It seems it was all meant to be.'

'Stop it, boy!' Grandad Abe cried.

'Oh, I will. Once you've all been dealt with!'

'Oculus!' It was Mum. 'There doesn't need to be any revenge.'

'I think you'll find there does!' the boy scoffed back at her.

'No, you're wrong,' Mum said. 'You were with us today. You saw Abe's office and all those photographs! He never abandoned you!'

'Rani's right!' Abe pleaded. 'I loved you, Oculus. I still do! I searched for years!'

Oculus threw his head back and practically screeched with laughter.

'You think I want revenge on **YOU?**' He snorted down at his father. **'HA!** I stopped caring about *you* a century ago! I'll admit I was surprised to discover you searched for us when I was rifling through your **REVOLTING** memories today, but that photograph means nothing to me and neither does your stupid pleading.'

'Then why are you doing this?' I shouted.

'**MAGICALS!**' Oculus roared, screwing up his face like the word tasted disgusting in his mouth. '**MAGICALS ARE THE REASON I'M LIKE THIS, AND I'M GOING TO MAKE YOU ALL PAY!**'

'No good can come from this, my wee lamb.' Nancy said as she clambered over the crowd from where she'd been watching near the carousel. 'It won't make things any better.'

'**BORING!**' Oculus mocked as he turned to head back into the tree-office. 'I think that's quite enough family time. Shall we get on with this?'

'I don't think so!' Maudlin grunted through gritted teeth, raising the wand again.

'Oh, don't you?' Oculus guffawed. He wriggled

his fingers in her direction and the wand flew straight out of her hand and into his. 'Finders keepers!'

## A SPECTRIL'S REVENGE!

Using his ghostly powers, Oculus snapped the wand in half and tossed it to the dance floor below.

'Now that everybody's down here together, it's time for the real party to begin!'

I watched with my heart pounding in my ears as my great-great-uncle crossed the high platform and stopped next to the perfumerator machine.

'Ooooh! I wonder what this does?' he jeered.

The spectril twitched his fingers at the cupboard of sea creature scents and it creaked slowly open.

'Hmmmm … These look like fun!'

'**NO!**' I yelled.

'What is it, Frankie?' Maudlin asked, panic spreading across her face.

'He can't use the machine!' I yelled. 'We have to stop him!'

I sprinted across the packed space to the gold symbol in the floor, then wracked my brains.

'What were the passwords!?!?'

Mum, Dad and Nancy clattered along behind me and were soon at my side.

'**OUTSIDE IN, DOWNSIDE OUT!**' I shouted, but nothing happened. '**INSIDE OUT, OUTSIDE DOWN!**' Dad joined in.

'**DOWNSIDE IN, INSIDE UP!**' tried Mum.

'Ugh! What is it?' I cried in frustration. I turned to glance at Oculus and saw that he'd magically wrenched the cage door from the bottom shelf and was laughing to himself as a small red jar was floating up towards the perfumerator.

'**WHAT AM I DOING!?**' Nancy suddenly blurted. 'I'm a spider! I don't need to use the lift!' The Orkney Brittle-back flung herself across the dance-floor towards the base of the tree, scattering guests in all directions. 'I'll stop him!'

'Keep trying, Frankie,' Dad said to me. 'Nancy

can't hold off a ghost and stop a machine at the same time.'

I mentally ran through all the different options in my head, and…

**'UPSIDE OUT, INSIDE DOWN!!!'**

Suddenly the shining tentacles started writhing under my feet, and just like before, they quickly lifted me high into the air and out across the room. 'There's something that's dying to meet you all!' Oculus cackled, as the bottle clicked into place at the base of the cannon. 'But what am I saying? It's you who'll be … oh, you get the picture!'

Nancy was hauling herself up over the edge of the tree-office and     my   toes

were just touching down on the mosaic floor when the perfumerator let rip with an almighty *BANG* and I watched in desperation as what looked like a red firework shot from the end of the machine's cannon and arched across the Briny Ballroom. It burst straight out through the bubble ceiling and exploded in a huge scarlet cloud above us.

The air inside the bubble filled with the foulest stench I think I've ever smelled. It was the stink of rotten fish and mould and decay.

'That wathn't tho bad!' I heard the Molar Sisters hooting to each other somewhere in the throng. 'Thmellth like bad breath! It'th quite nithe!'

'Was that it?' Reginald Blink smirked from the staircase as he held his nose. 'That bratly boy thought he'd scare us all to death with a smelly firework!'

'What drivel and snotlishness!' Berol Dunch shouted as she swam overhead.

'No!' I yelled over the room. 'You don't understand…'

But the hundreds of guests started laughing and

going back to their partying. The anemenonk orchestra started playing again.

'What monster have you called?' I growled at my great-great-uncle. 'Tell me!'

Oculus shrugged and grinned.

'Can't remember!' He sniggered. 'But you'll soon find out.'

'You tell us what you're up to, you wee jobby, or I'll waft you into ghosty globs! I've got a lot of hands!!' shouted Nancy.

'Do it, spider!' Oculus chuckled. 'You can't hurt me. I'm safely frozen on the other side of the world, remember?'

Trying to talk to my bonkers uncle was completely useless. Anyone with half a brain could see that. I ran to the perfumerator to look for any clues of what Oculus had done.

'The jar is still here!' I shouted to Nancy, yanking it out.

'What scent was in there, Frankie?' asked Nancy.

'I wouldn't even want to know if I were you,' Oculus teased.

'It's…' I could feel my hands trembling as I raised the little red container and turned it over in my palm. 'Gundiskump!'

The book I'd been reading earlier today swam to the front of my memory and my legs turned to jelly beneath me. I wobbled to the railing and looked down at my parents and Maudlin who were right below on the dance floor.

**'IT'S A GUNDISKUMP!!'** I screamed as loud as I could, and everyone froze in their tracks. There wasn't a single magical in the whole ocean who hadn't heard the terrible tales of these dreadful beasts, and I could see heart-stopping fear on all their faces.

I was about to yell, **'GET OUT OF HERE!'** but Oculus whooshed past me and flew high into the air above the tree.

**'NOBODY MOVE!'** the spectril bellowed, and as quickly as he brandished his arms above his head, I started to hear yelps and cries of fear as mercreatures darted away from the bubble walls.

I looked up in horror to see that, outside, in a

circle surrounding the entire ballroom, was an army of skeleton mermaid warriors. They were clutching long rusted forks and spears and they gnashed their rotten teeth menacingly.

'**BOO!**' Oculus squealed with delight, singing like he was reciting a nursery rhyme. 'I've got you surrounded!'

The bony mermaidens slowly swam in through the walls and everybody huddled tighter and tighter together, trying their best to get away from the rancid things. Their spiny tails and gnarled ribs dripped with slime, and the hair growing from their skulls was a mass of tangled seaweed.

'Did you all forget about my powers?' Oculus laughed. 'If it's dead, it works for me. Ha ha! No one is leaving until our guest of honour arrives. Isn't that right, disgusting daughters of the deep?'

The mermaids all gurgled a sickening squelchy laugh.

'Oh…' Oculus trilled, pointing into the depths beyond the coral garden outside. 'And it looks like we won't have to wait too long.'

## GUNDISKUMP!

It started as a faint blue glow in the darkness, dimming and then brightening as it got closer.

'I bet it's hungry!' Oculus cackled. 'Who's first? Any volunteers?'

Nobody made a sound. We watched in petrified silence as the strange flickering blob grew nearer and nearer. I didn't seem to be able to take my eyes away from it. Even the gristly mermaids had twisted their grinning heads to watch it through their empty eye-sockets.

'Oooh, it's a big one!!'

The glimmering shape was gliding high over the pleasure garden now and in only a matter of seconds would be right outside the bubble.

'Who's wants a fish supper?' Oculus cheered. 'Sorry … who wants to *be* a fish's supper? Ha ha!'

Eerie and graceful, the glowing orb stopped just beyond the ballroom walls and bobbed there gently. It was about the size of the great big inflatable beach balls they sell at the end of Brighton Pier, and no matter how hard I tried, I couldn't do anything but stare. I couldn't even blink.

A feeling of calm passed over me and I felt a massive urge to head towards it.

The only person it didn't seem to have any effect on was Maudlin Maloney, and it was her voice that rang across the ballroom, breaking everyone's half-trance. It felt like the world had suddenly rushed back in through my eyes and ears!

**'NOT ON YOUR NELLY!'** she hollered and threw a tiny talisman from her charms pouch at the nearest skeleton mermaid, which instantly crumbled to dust. Its rusted spear clattered to the floor and before any of the other undead guards could stop her, Maudlin snatched it up and hurled the pointed thing at the shimmering blue blob on the other side of the bubble walls.

There was a thunderous rumbly roar as the weapon hit its target and thousands of fibrous feelers that snaked down the grotesque monster's face suddenly illuminated in the blackness!

I'm not sure I could ever properly describe the monster that flashed into view before us, my reader friend, even if I tried for the rest of my life.

The gundiskump was as big as the ballroom's bubble itself and the glowing blob we'd all been gawping at was wiggling about on the end of a stalk that grew out of the creature's forehead. Its mouth was stuffed full of sabre-like teeth that were as long as the Under-Oak was tall. I swear to you, there was an entire wrecked ship skewered on one of the

Its four yellow eyes were streaked with purple veins and were the size of the giant sun umbrellas that stand around the pool-deck back at the hotel.

The scales around its blubbery lips and gills undulated with scars and lumps. I could see hundreds of harpoons and anchors wedged between them. It was a horror to behold, and every bit of the ghastly beast pulsated and throbbed with a sickly orange light.

'**RUN!**' Maudlin wailed, reaching into her charms purse and lobbing whatever trinkets she'd thrown before. More skeleton mermaids burst into clouds of dust and that was enough to send the crowd of trapped magicals into a frenzy of movement.

'Flee! Flee! Flee!' a mergully cried as she sped through the air over my head and vanished into the darkness on the far side of the bubble.

'**RETREAT!**' the swelkies bellowed and in a single line, they sped out though the ballroom walls, click-clacking as they went.

The Gundiskump seemed as hypnotised by all the movement inside the bubble as we'd been by its lure. It flapped its fins and rose slightly, so that it was looking down on us from above.

'Get to the Atilantus!' I heard the real Abe yelling to any non-mermagical, as people tore across the dancefloor.

The hippocamps that had been tied up near the fountains broke their harnesses then galloped off in different directions, braying and snorting. They bolted into the outside waters, and ... in all their panic ... one of them raced straight towards the Gundiskump!

There was an enormous gulp and that's when things got really ... umm ... interesting...

## THE RACE TO DRY LAND

With a taste of warm food, the Gundiskump started its attack.

Four whip-like feelers snaked into the bubble and started snatching at people as they darted about. It definitely wasn't a picky eater, let me tell you.

The first things to go were several daughters of the deep. The skeleton maidens wailed and screeched as the glowing feelers suddenly snared them by their tales and **SWOOSH,** down the creature's throat they went, spears and all.

'This is my cue to say **"TA-TA!"'** Oculus sneered at me and Nancy as chaos clattered around beneath us. 'I hate to leave, but this

party is **DEAD!'**

**'OH, NO, YOU DON'T!'** Abe grunted as he sped up into the branches of the Under-Oak. 'You're forgetting who your father is, boy! I know a thing or two about spectrils, and I know what happens if you're touched by a real ghost!'

Abe reached out and grabbed his son's wrist.

**'GET OFF!'** Oculus howled, but it was too late. No sooner had Abe's ghostly grip touched the boy's flesh, Oculus's spectril dissolved into a yellow and fizzing cloud. **'NOOOOOOOOOOO!'**

'Quick! Don't let the spectril float away!' Abe yelled to Nancy. 'Get the jar with the pickled pamplemoogs in it! It's phantom-proofed!'

'Right you are, Abe!' Nancy cooed, grabbing the glass container and emptying its contents over the floor. Then, in one swift movement, she caught the little cloud as it swirled over Abe's head, and clamped on the lid. **'GOT YOU!'**

Oculus was furious with rage! The ball of fog twisted and whirled inside its see-through prison and although we couldn't spot any sign of my

loop-de-loop crazy uncle among the streams and
curls of smoke, we could hear his curses echoing
around the inside of the jar.

'Frankie! Nancy! Abraham!' a voice
called from below. It was Mum. I
looked down and saw her
hurdle over one of the
Gundiskump's feelers as it
swung in a huge arc across
the floor. '**WE
HAVE TO GO
NOW!**'

'She's right,
my wee beauty!'
Nancy huffed at
me. Tucking the glass jar
under one of her arms, our
spider-chef scooped me up
with her others and lowered
me over the side of the office platform.

'A bit more,' I called up to her when
my feet were nearly at the floor.

'Just a bit mo…'

*CRAAAAAAAAAAAAAAAAAAAA*
*AAAAAAAAAAASSSSSSSSSHHHHHHH!!*

Another of the sea monster's feelers lashed through the bubble walls and thumped into the Under-Oak, toppling it instantly.

There was an ear-splitting squeal and I was thrown halfway across the dance floor with Nancy skidding painfully along beside me as the tree was splintered into shards of scrap metal.

'This way!' Dad's arm was suddenly around my waist and he dragged me back to my feet. 'Are you hurt? Can you run, Frankie?'

'I'm fine,' I shouted above the din of the helter-skelter collapsing. '**GO, GO, GO!!**'

Nancy clambered back to her feet and was clattering along next to us in seconds. We sprinted towards the Atilantus station at the top of the looping staircases, and the last of the mergullies and kulpies wailed through the air.

'**GET OUT OF THE WAY!**' Nancy barked at a skeleton mermaid who darted into our path, brandishing a trident. The ghastly thing hissed at us and raked a dark green tongue over its jagged teeth. She raised her weapon above her head, and I was just about to grit my eyes tight and wait for the impact of it when a glowing tendril smashed down on top of her only a footstep's breadth in front of us. 'Jump! We're almost there!'

Me and Dad dived over the flattened mermaid bones and tore up the cracking steps, two and three at a time, while Nancy practically cleared them all in one leap.

'Quick!' yelled Dad, grabbing at a home-sweet-home-hob who was desperately trying to sweep up the remains of a smashed statue with its little dustpan and brush. 'Let's get out of here!'

Mum and a gaggle of our regular guests were waiting for us at the top and we all piled into the only Atilantus carriage that hadn't rocketed off to dry land already.

'GO! GO! GO!' Mum screamed. '**START THE ENGINE!**'

Gingiva Molar slapped her tiny hand over the

green glowing button just as Grandad Abe materialised in the seat next to her with a small shower of ectoplasm.

He instantly spun around to all of us sitting in the rows behind as clouds of steam started to billow out of the sides of the fish-shaped machine.

'Hello! It's lovely to finally meet you,' he huffed to us all. 'But, where's Oculus? Who has the jar?'

I looked up at Nancy and caught sight of her face twisting with shock.

'Och, no!'

'Where is it?' Grandad Abe barked.

**'BLUNKING BLUNKERS!** I've dropped it!' Nancy sobbed. The Atilantus started rattling on the spot, revving itself up for blast off. 'It's too late now!'

'We can't leave it!' Abe replied. 'He'll escape again!'

And that right there, just as the Atilantus suddenly lurched forward, was the moment I dived out of my seat back onto the station platform and watched as my family hurtled out of the Briny

Ballroom with my mum's screams echoing in my ears...

**'FRAAANNNKKKIIIEEE!!!'**

## KA-BOOM!

There was no time to lose! I had to find the glass jar with great-great-uncle Oculus's spectril inside ... then figure out a way of getting back to dry land without being eaten by a sea monster!

'Frankie Banister, you **BLUNKING BLUNDER- BRAIN!**' I hollered at myself as I ran back down the curvy staircase, trying to keep my head low.

The daughters of the deep seemed to have changed their minds after their leader was locked up in a jar, and now the remaining few were battling the Gundiskump themselves, which was a pretty honkhumptious distraction.

This was my chance. As the skeletons poked

and jabbed their spears at the monster's feelers that slapped this way and that across the floor and up the walls, I darted over to the wreckage of the Under-Oak and started yanking great pieces of twisted metal aside.

'Where is it?' I groaned, hauling more and more of the broken branches away. 'Where is it?'

I found part of the mummified hinkapoot chieftain **(BLEURGH!)**, the clay nomad mask that had given me the chills, and a very squashed prattle-peacer machine, but I couldn't see the glass urn anywhere.

Yanking up more and more debris, I lifted a sheet of silver bark and discovered the crumbled remains of the tiny house we'd seen hours ago. There huddled in one of the nearly flattened window-boxes was Viscera Von Tangle.

'Banister boy!' she squeaked, as she glanced up blinking in the bright light of the Gundiskump's glow. 'The old ghost! It's a spectril!'

'Yep! We figured that out already, Mistress Von Tangle.'

'Then save me, you idiot!'

There was no time left to think. Grabbing the piskie princess by the scruff of her dress, I plucked her into the air like she was one of Nancy's crab-curd koftas and dropped her into my jacket pocket.

I was just about to dive back into the wreckage and try to burrow deeper, when I heard scratchy screaming coming from behind me. For the teensiest of seconds, I thought it might be Oculus cursing and howling inside his new prison, and I spun around.

'Go on, my girlies!'

It definitely wasn't my bonkers uncle...

Flapping around her lepre-caravan like she'd gone around the twist, Maudlin Maloney

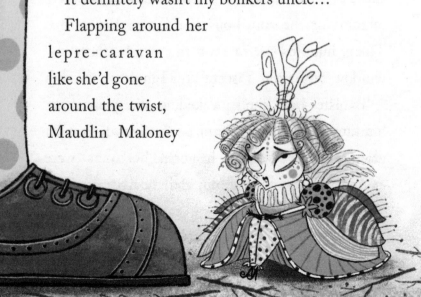

was running in circles throwing lucky charms at her pet chickens.

'Be off wit' yer!' she barked. 'Go now!'

'Maudlin!' I ran across the dance floor, hurdling great pieces of the balconies and the giant gold claws that held the walls in place. Everything was starting to fall apart!

The ancient leprechaun glanced my way for a split-second.

'Oh, it's you…' she grunted over her shoulder.

'Maudlin, we have to find the glass jar and get out of here!'

'Why bother?' she snapped. 'No one cares for Manky Old Maloney! No one checks I'm safe before they rocket off on their fishmobile!'

'I'm here, aren't I?'

'Not the same!' she yelled, then went back to what she was doing, throwing charms at her chickens. I watched as each little silver trinket hit their mark and, one by one, her pets were surrounded by a bubble and floated upwards towards the surface of the ocean. 'Float away, me darlings! Me lovely wifelings!'

*CRUUUUUUNCH!*

Another enormous piece of the golden claws collapsed, demolishing the carousel and half the food trucks.

'Maudlin!' I screamed, turning to see the last of the skeleton mermaids vanishing down the Gundiskumps gaping gullet. 'We have to go!'

'I'm not leavin' me winksome lepre-caravan!' Maloney wailed. 'Me spells! Me beautiful curses!'

'We have no choice! Come on!'

'Ah, **BOG OFF**, Frankie Banister, and leave me with my trinks and tatts!'

Maudlin threw a charm at the final hen and it was instantly encased in a football-sized bubble. We both watched as it drifted off, following the others.

'Good luck to you, my Henelope!' Maudlin cried. 'Remember me!'

From down here, the escaping chickens looked like someone had let go of a whole bunch of feathery and very noisily clucking balloons.

**BOOOOOOOOM!**

One side of the staircase to the Atilantus station cracked in two and fell into the fountains.

It was now or never…

'Maudlin! Forget the jar!' I shouted. 'Can you put us in a bubble like your chickens?'

Maloney turned and looked at me like I'd gone loop-de-loop insane.

'Don't be brain-mangled, boy! Those were chicken-bubble charms … for chickens! You don't think I just go skittering about all day with a caravan full of boy-bubble charms or leprechaun-bubble charms, do you? What **BLUNKING NONKUMBUMPS!!!'**

This was useless! Without saying another word, I grabbed Maloney by the wrist and ran for it. If we could reach the Atilantus platform, we might be able to follow the track-tunnels all the way back to the Nothing To See Here Hotel.

'**GET OFF!**' Maudlin howled, but I refused to let go. We would never have survived my great-great-uncle's first attempt at destroying us if it hadn't been for her, and I wasn't about to let her get eaten by a Gundiskump now.

'Not much further!' I called over my shoulder as I sprinted, yanking the hobbling leprechaun along behind me. 'Don't stop!'

We darted around fallen objects and jumped over the wide cracks that had suddenly appeared in the floor. If we didn't reach the tunnels sharpish, we'd be goners for certain. The whole place was crumbling in on top of us.

Just as we reached the base of the stairs, there was an ear-shattering squeal of metal and wood, and we turned to see Maudlin's lepre-caravan being dragged across the trembling floor as one of the monster's glowing feelers snaked through the spokes of the brightly painted wheels.

'**MY HOME!!!**' Maloney wailed.

Neither of us moved.

With the Briny Ballroom raining down

around us, we watched in horror as the Gundiskump shoved its grotesque face through the walls, glowing and pulsating and belching great gusts of foul-smelling breath as it came.

Water began surging in on all sides as the enchanted bubble started to tear and a voice inside my head whispered, *He's won! Oculus Nocturne has won!*

Frozen in fright, the pair of us stood there and stared as Maloney's caravan was dragged between the Gundiskump's nightmarish teeth.

It was like everything was moving in slow motion!

My memories of what happened next are a little bit hazy, but I'll do my best to remember, my reader friend.

Just as the sea monster's giant teeth began to close around the ancient leprechaun's home, she turned to me with wide eyes and…

'There are armfuls of deadlish dangery things in there!' she shrieked. **'GET DOWN!'**

The world slowed even more as the Gundiskump

chomped onto the little wooden caravan and it **EXPLODED** in the most tremendous blast of magical green and purple flames.

Giant lumps of rancid fish hurtled across the entire ballroom and … **THE BUBBLE WALLS CAVED IN!**

Crushing waters from outside came surging towards us. I grabbed Maloney and hurled her up the stairs and we ran, tripping and stumbling, but I knew it was no use. There was no way we could out sprint, tonnes of cascading sea water.

'Goodbye, boy!' Maloney cried. 'I'll see you in the Land of the D—'

Time sped up in an instant as I spotted the yellow knitted hat with blue trim and a red pom-pom laying on the step above us. Without a second to think, I yanked the soggy thing onto my head and just had time to wrap my arms around Maudlin's little waist, before…

**'WHOOOOOOOOMMMMMMFFFFFF!'**

## THAT'S THAT THEN . . .

**YOU MADE IT ALL THE WAY TO THE END OF THE STORY, MY HUMAN FRIEND!!**

I told you it was good'un, didn't I?

Everything that happened after me and Manky Old Maloney went shooting up out of the ocean like a four-armed, two-headed screeching torpedo with a nice woollen hat on is a complete blur.

All I remember is the sound of Mum's voice echoing like it was miles and miles away, and the feeling of Hoggit licking my face with his little paws on my chest.

My family found me on Brighton beach, twisted

in seaweed and stinking of Gundiskump guts, while Maudlin washed up not too far away with the octopus who'd been flipping pancakes knotted up in her dreadlocks and twenty chickens in bubbles clucking in circles around her.

Hearing her croaking: **'GET THIS SQUIDGLY THING OFF ME!'** will forever be one of the loveliest sounds I think I've ever heard … **HA HA!**

Once we'd both been carried back to the hotel, wrapped in blankets and given mug after steaming mug of pondweed tea from Nancy, I started to feel a bit more like my old self. The fact that Mum gave me a whole month off from chores for being brave also helped a bit!

**BUT!** That's not the even best news, because…

## DRUM ROLL, PLEASE!!!

Among all the debris and chunks of Gundiskump that washed up alongside me and Maloney, we spotted a particular glass jar bobbing about in the shadows under the pier. Well … **'WE'** isn't quite right ... it was Great-Great-Great-Grandad Abraham who found it. The **REAL** Great-Great-Great-Grandad Abraham! He used his ghost senses and located his evil son's spiteful spectril in no time.

With Oculus's body frozen in the Himalayas, and his soul trapped in a glass jar on the opposite side of the world, it looked like he wouldn't be bothering us any time soon. Dad was instructed to store the spectril on one of the highest shelves in the library with all the really old **BORING** books for now. No one will disturb it there.

And so ... that's that.

Just another average day in **the Nothing To See Here Hotel!**

Ooof built poor Maudlin and her chickens a little house in the garden by the compost heap, a very bedraggled Princess Viscera Von Tangle has moved into one of the kitchen cupboards, and Grandad Abe has been staying on the three hundred and ninety-nine steps that lead up to

Granny Regurgita's bedroom. Every night when I take the demented rhinoceros her dinner, he's outside her door singing love songs through the keyhole.

She absolutely hates it, but it serves her right for being such a grumpy grunion!

Anyway ... don't stay away too long, my reader friend.

If you think what happened today was crazy, you'll pop your clonkers when you hear what happened next at The Nothing To See Here Hotel, where weird is the new normal.

See you next time!

Steven Butler

**Steven B** is an award-winning children's writer, actor, voice artist and host of World Book Day's The Biggest Book Show On Earth. When not typing, twirling about on stage, or being very dramatic on screen, Steven spends his time trying to spot thistlewumps at the bottom of the garden and catching dust pooks in jars. His *The Wrong Pong* series was shortlisted for the prestigious Roald Dahl Funny Prize.

**www.stevenbutlerbooks.com**

**Steven L** is an award-winning illustrator based in Brighton, not far from *The Nothing To See Here Hotel*! As well as designing all of the creatures you have just seen throughout this book, Steven also illustrates the *Shifty McGifty and Slippery Sam* series and Frank Cottrell Boyce's fiction titles. When he isn't drawing giant spiders and geriatric mermaids, Steven loves to eat ice cream on Brighton beach looking out for goblin pirate ships on the horizon.

**www.stevenlenton.com**

Steven Lenton

# THE NOTHING to see HERE
# ★★★ HOTEL ★★★